I0781458

Pit Stop

Ellis Mae

Pit Stop
Copyright © 2024 by Ellis Mae
All rights reserved.

This is a work of fiction. All of the characters, organizations, and events in this novel are products of the author's imagination or used fictitiously. Any resemblance to actual events, or locales, or persons living or dead, is entirely coincidental.

Ellismaewriting.com
Instagram.com: ellismaewriting

First Edition

Author's Note

Throughout life, we are met with many hardships. Although this book ends happily, it comes with hardships of its own. The story follows a military veteran with PTSD and a transfemoral amputation, as well as an overworked college student taking care of his father—a recovering alcoholic.

If at any point you discover these scenes are too much for you, I implore you to simply put the book down. Life is hard enough, but I wrote this book hoping it will bring you peace.

To my parents and to Duke Gardens where they spent hours walking with me every summer. It helped me grow my imagination and, for that, I can never be thankful enough

Chapter One

John

IF I COULD BURY MYSELF in the North Carolina soil, made for dense forests of trees, I would. Anything to get out of meeting Aaliyah's new boyfriend. He has the hair on the back of my neck standing at attention. My leg craves to bounce in place, but I sit stiffly on his too clean couch.

"Aaliyah says you're really into photography," Gonzales says with an easy smile that reminds me he's a psychology major.

I feel like a small child sitting across from him.

There's a beer can in front of me gathering condensation, but none of my fingerprints, and I feel like Gonzales has been taking note of it. It's a local brew I don't recognize, but I'm sure my pa would know the name.

Aaliyah raises her eyebrow at me. It's a sign to behave, it's a sign to breathe. It's both because she knows I hate Gonzales, even though I've never met him until now.

"Is that a bad question?" he asks when my silence goes on for too long.

It isn't that it's a bad question necessarily. It's that the question involves telling him about my dad and about how young and naïve I once was. I began taking photos to spare my dad from missing out on things while he was away on deployment. Jokes on me, of course, because he ended up missing everything.

"Just collecting memories," I finally tell him, sitting back and smiling calmly.

The entire façade only shows what I want it to. Let him falsely think I'm sentimental and not masochistic.

"Okay," he replies, mouth quirked at the corner to let me know he's letting me get away with my half-truth. Psych majors are a burden to society. I've told my therapist as much.

Aaliyah sees right past our cock show and diverts Gonzales's focus onto her as she talks about my photography. Nothing divulging; just small talk between new acquaintances that she shoulders so I don't have to.

I exhale the weight of dealing with Aaliyah's new boyfriend. The pit in my stomach is heavy, feeling nothing but anger. It's good that Aaliyah is dating, it's good that she feels comfortable enough about our friendship that she can bring other people into it. At least, that's what my therapist says. I see it as another way for the universe to prove no one will stay by my side.

There have been two people in my life that have unexpectedly slipped into the circle of things I care about. Aaliyah is one of them. That's the only reason I'm even here, trying to not let her slip through my fingers before it's too late.

I roll my shoulders, trying to push back my toxic thoughts and discomfort.

Unfortunately, I can see why Aaliyah likes him. He looks like an uncut stone, sturdy and reliable in a way that her family has never been. He looks like he could cut out our hearts neatly and put them on a display case. Aaliyah likes that sort of honesty and openness in a man. I detest it.

"Are you planning on taking photos for the Trans Rights Rally? It's all Aaliyah talks about," Gonzales says earnestly, and I immediately fight back an eye roll.

Aaliyah told me they met in a local bookstore, hands touching as they both reached for a memoir in the queer section. Their meet-cute does little to sway my opinion of him. For all I know, he could've been grabbing it for a report on why being queer is a mental illness.

"Of course it's all I talk about," Aaliyah starts. "How could you not think about how people in our country are fighting for their rights?"

"Yeah, I know what you mean. My mom came here looking for the American dream and… well, life hardly works out that way for migrants," Gonzales says, his thick eyebrows turning down into a frown. "Politicians are just uneducated figureheads. I've taken a few queer education courses for the psychology track, since one day it'll be my job to approve folks for gender affirming care and—" he sighs. "If they just took an introductory course, I feel like things would be different."

I hum in agreement, but in reality, I'm exhausted. Aaliyah and I have spent the entire beginning of the semester trying to organize this rally. There are schedules to consider and approval to be obtained. I've been involved in as much activism as I can on campus these past two years. Being an activist has only resulted in single-minded conversations, where everyone postures in a game of trying to prove themselves the best ally. It's as if gaining my approval means their own bigotry is excused.

I'm sure Gonzales is just like everyone else trying to earn his gold star. His apartment is uncomfortably clean and tidy. The fridge is stocked with nice beer and fresh veggies. If this is what college men were really like, I might have actually dated someone by now.

His pristine brown-nosing still makes me feel underdressed in my oil-stained shirt, but it was either this or a date shirt. I try to only use those late at night when the loneliness of sharing a bed solely with textbooks sets in and Grindr starts to look like a good option.

I eye the unopened beer on the table with distaste and think about my dad, who I should've already been with by now. I've been here too long watching Gonzales and Aaliyah snuggle up together.

"Well, it's been great meeting you," I lie. "But I have to head out." I stand and clasp hands with Gonzales.

"Hold on, I'll walk you out," Aaliyah says, standing up quickly.

She walks me all the way to my car, which by this point is basically a family heirloom. The clutch sticks between first and second, I have to pull the handle twice before the driver side door even opens, and the seats have stains of my father's past indiscretions, but it's my car. My dad's car. The car. The Love Family Car.

"He's a good guy, John," Aaliyah says, seeing past everything everyone else does.

I shrug. "He seems like a guy you'd like." I turn and give her a hug, minding her afro that fills me with envy. Even in the North Carolina humidity, it never falters.

"Ringing approval," she says, voice dripping with sarcasm.

Aaliyah and I have known each other since our freshman year at Duke University—a chance encounter during club sign ups where we both reached for the pen at the same time. The rest is a series of late nights studying with breaks in between to decorate protest signs. Neither of us have the best relationships with our families, but we've done our best to look out for each other.

"He's a senior, Liyah. He's just going to be gone next year." I don't tell her I also don't trust him. She knows that already. I don't trust people further than I can throw them. "But, if he makes you happy…"

She nods and rests her head against my shoulder.

"A'ite," she mumbles against me, using a word she's stolen from my own southern vocabulary. "Thanks for coming. I know you've got other things to be doing."

"Work," I tell her with an eye roll, even though we both know that's only a half-truth. I already worked my double shift.

She turns away, back to Gonzales's, and I pull the car door handle twice until it pops open.

The car smells like air fresheners, so much so that it's nearly pungent, in an attempt to cover the smell of spilled booze that's accumulated over the years. It's worse as I press my forehead against the steering wheel, nose too close to the scent clipped onto the vents.

"Please don't be dead. Please don't be dead. Please don't be dead." But after repeating the mantra enough times, it begins to blend and go fuzzy at the edges until I'm not sure it doesn't sound like "please be dead".

I start the car and the engine roars to life. Even if I've never gotten this old gal a paint job, it's not the car that I'm worried about dying; she still runs smoother than butter. I start my long and quiet drive to my alcoholic dad's mobile home, filled with broken memories of absent parents.

North Carolina doesn't care about what weather it brings. It doesn't care to make the beaches bright and sunny throughout the months when tourists flock in, or make the mountains snow covered for ski season. Sometimes, in the summer, when I'm trying to get my dad out of the house and into the sun, North Carolina will choose that day to be overcast—trapping in the humidity and chasing away any hopes of Vitamin-C. Sometimes, in the winter, that same humidity will spike, and I'll feel like my shirt has been soaked into my skin, only to then freeze against my already aching body.

Every summer, no matter if the highways are being expanded or if the campuses are suddenly desolate, the cicadas crawl out of their trees and scream all day in search of a mate, until the fireflies replace them at night. Although, there have been less and less of their light each year. Every autumn, the trees in the Appalachians blossom across the mountains in yellows and oranges that send people flocking to take photos, myself included. Every winter, we play a game of cat and mouse with the snow to see if it'll come—it hardly ever does in Durham.

Every spring, it rains.

It rains so abruptly and heavily that sometimes it'll catch you by surprise while driving on I-85. The downpour can be so aggressive that the hood of the car isn't even visible. It was one of these storms that killed my mother over eleven years ago.

North Carolina doesn't care about emotions. Because, despite the ocean of wonder and mystery—its cities brimming with excitement and opportunity, its mountains vivid with life and adventure—it still didn't hold me, not in the great branches of the trees above me as I cried. Its roots never erupted from the ground to take me away, like I so often begged. The leaves never fell in quantities so great that it would cover the tears I had shed.

It's because I was raised by North Carolina that I try to care so little. A false attempt to be like the enigma of beasts that crawl in between the dark shadows cast by trees. Like the tumultuous weather that rains and cries all at once before suddenly stopping, hiding it all behind a sunny sky. I am the years and years of war and blood held in this land.

I don't blame my parents for growing up halfway between a

trailer home and a military base. I don't blame my dad for joining the army in an effort to better our lives so we could get out of that trailer home. I don't blame my mom for dying in a tragic car accident while my dad was across the world.

That doesn't mean they're completely blameless for how shit my childhood was.

Addiction is a disease. Logically, I understand that, but it's different when you're ten years old staring at your sweaty, puke-covered dad laying on the floor. The same floor where your recently deceased mom once twirled around in time with the spinning vinyl records.

His temporary leave was supposed to be about handling the situation and taking me back with him until his contract was up. Instead, I had to handle him. Only to be abandoned to the lonely trailer and a wallowing aunt as he finished up his contract, alone and drunk.

Thick branches of trees—an eternal prison of bad memories—open up to a trailer park, gravel crunching under my already bare tires.

The trailer still has its lights on when I pull up making a shiver run down my spine.

After my dad's contract was up and we returned to North Carolina, I knew exactly what I was coming home to every day—an empty house with the promise of booze behind every corner. My dad used to come home late at night, if at all, and pass out on the couch or call for me as he puked in our kitchen sink, only to rinse and repeat every night after he got off work.

Now he's home every day, except for when his AA buddy drives him to their shared job. When I open that door, he could still be puking or passed out on the couch—or worse. Now, it isn't because he's drunk. It's because he spent so much time being drunk that he's permanently destroyed his liver.

It always takes me a minute to gather the courage to open the door and I avoid it by walking over to the old 1969 Camaro—once bright red, now a rusted brown—and lean against it.

There's a couple of empty bottles of booze sitting in it. But once, it was our dream car. My dad bought it before his final deployment. He'd promised me, my chubby face in his cupped hands, that when he came back, we'd fix it up. He just didn't know he would come back to an empty house, and I would come back from my aunt's house to an empty father.

Staring at the broken shambles of my childhood, I snap a photo on the other camera I carry with me—a dinky little Polaroid. It's a continuation of my masochistic streak that reminds me that this is all that's left.

Steeling myself, I walk up the stairs and through the door. My dad is on the couch, sipping on a bottle of sparkling water. I heard they're good for staving off the urge to drink and now we have enough supplies to last us a year.

"How was your night?" he asks, looking back at me.

This is when a good son smiles. This is when a good son says, "thank you for leaving the lights on and waiting to make sure I got home safe." This is when a good son gives his ailing father a hug.

I'm not a good son.

But only because my dad was never a good father.

"It was fine," I respond, going to the fridge and counting the meal prepped dishes still left.

Every Sunday, I make my dad's food for the week and try to gauge what he can actually stomach on his weak appetite. It'd be easier if he just told me.

My dad calls me from the couch, where he's cradled in his cable knit cardigan, and pats the spot beside him. I reluctantly sit beside him.

"You eat enough?" I ask as SportsCenter blares on the TV.

"Yeah," he says proudly.

I let the silence between us hold his lie so I don't have to.

He sighs.

I sigh.

"I took my meds but it's still hard to eat," he tells me, excitement drained from his voice. "Sorry," he adds quietly.

I pat his leg. It's frail beneath my palm. "I know, dad. At least you ate something. I have work in the morning."

Despite everything, it still hurts to see him as ill as he is.

"Okay. Take the keys to bed with you or I'll run to the ABC," he says. "I had a bad customer today and it's been really gettin' to me," he explains.

I look down at him as I stand from the couch. His brown eyes are the same as mine, full of grief and sorrow for a life that could've been.

When I was little, I looked like my mom. The same round face and untamable head of spiral curls. Now I look like my dad. I don't know which is worse.

"A'ite," I say, taking the keys from him. My tongue rolls in my mouth uncomfortably. I know I'm supposed to say something supportive, but I wouldn't even know where to start.

He gives me a sad smile and I walk away from him to my bedroom. Unlocking it, I immediately collapse into bed, too tired to care.

It's too late to try and give a shit. It's always been too late.

Isamu

The Raleigh/Durham international airport is surprisingly small for being an academic hub, since it only takes Inu and I a few dozen yards before we're at the escalator for the exit gates. I'm thankful for the short distance as I shift my backpack and medical bag to alleviate pressure off my prosthetic limb.

Inu presses against me calmly, unaffected by the grinding metal of the escalator below us.

Despite that I just spent two weeks learning Inu's commands beside her trainers, her behavior still impresses me. A service rottweiler made for sturdiness that I've named Inu, much to Japanese parents' horror.

Inu must feel my gaze on her because her heavy brown eyes look up into my nearly black ones. I rub her head as we exit the airport and enter a muggy North Carolina day—typical for the area but unwelcome nonetheless.

I had to wait a few months after my medical separation from the army to get her because I went to visit my mom in Japan. Now I'm back, and I've trapped Inu with me in a city where no one even needs me anymore. My mom is across the world, my dad is selling our childhood home to join her, and my best friend is less than a year from graduation.

"No *mames*. Look what the devil dragged in," Gonzales shouts, arms wide open from where he's been loitering in the arrival lane.

"Holy shit," I call out, grin splitting my face as I move forward and clutch Gonzales tightly in my fatigued arms—traveling on a plane is truly the worst. Between the heavy medical bag and swelling of my residual limb from altitude, I think I'll be swearing off planes for the rest of my life.

I hold onto Gonzales like a lifeline. Like a long-lost brother.

"Fuck, did you get taller?" I clasp his shoulder, ashamed I have to look so far up to meet his eyes.

"Nah, Isa, I think you got shorter. You sure you didn't lose both legs?"

I cackle as he takes my medical bag off my shoulder. He groans under the weight of it before turning back toward us.

"Is this her?" he whispers with reverie, lowering himself to eye level with Inu, who obediently ignores him.

When the VA said I qualified for a service animal because of my above knee amputation and PTSD, both resulting in a heart condition, I figured I'd get a labrador to carry my ass home from a drunken night out. Turns out, they kind of throw you into group therapy during your two years before medical retirement to see if you've even got the mental functionality to be worthy of a dog.

"No. This is just some dog I picked up in a dark alley of Shibuya." I give him a deadpan look and drop my backpack between them. "Yeah, this is Inu. Don't pet her though."

Gonzales lets out a snort of laughter. "I thought Takeo was joking when he said you named your dog 'Dog'."

I shrug and open the back seat of Gonzales's flashy muscle car, then usher Inu in before opening the passenger door for myself. I don't know much about cars, but I know a Mustang when I see one and I know a flashy car if it's got electric blue racing stripes on white like this.

"Where'd you get the money for this bad boy?" I ask, staring at the interior—too flashy for me to understand.

"Sued my mom after my sister moved out," he grumbles while he loads my bag into the backseat. "Sorry, didn't want to bring it up with everything going on in your life. It was just after I visited you in the hospital."

I frown at him as he gets in the driver's side. "Fuck that. You know you could've told me. I would've been here for you as much as I could." I don't comment on the bitter hurt that fills me knowing he didn't need my support anymore. Not like when we were kids. "Glad you won though."

He grabs my shoulder. "Yeah, I know. But I also kind of enjoyed you not seeing that side of me. Turns out I'm a bit of an asshole when it comes to getting my due diligence."

"You're always an asshole," I tell him sweetly. "Smells like a chick in here." Even my seatbelt has hints of perfume on it as I buckle in.

"*Culero*, I told you I'm seeing someone," Gonzales complains. He pops me on the back of the head.

I take a pointed sniff and look at him only to be met with an uncaring glance. Gonzales always made fun of me for blushing so easily. I've tried to make him blush at any opportunity I get.

"You tell her you love her yet?"

"You get your first kiss yet?" he shoots back.

He knows I have. In the basement of his mom's house during a middle school party where we pretended the Bojangles sweet tea was spiked. I told him it didn't count because I wasn't even dating the girl, and he's held it over my head ever since.

By middle school standards: I still have not, despite all the men I've kissed and slept with.

Gonzales laughs as soon as my cheeks flare up. Despite my embarrassment, it feels good to be here again with my best friend.

Sometimes, I wish Gonzales would have gone to Afghanistan with me. Then I remember Smith holding me down as Doc sawed my leg off to get me out from under the rubble, and I change my mind. Gonzales doesn't deserve any more pain in his life.

"How's my old man?" I ask once we hit the highway, hands clawing at the seatbelt constricting me—we're driving too fast to be on the lookout for IEDs.

Gonzales grunts an affirmative and goes on to tell me my dad gave him a B- in introduction to political science. The sound of Gonzales's complaints does nothing to deter my swiveling head. Since he's not looking for IEDs, I'm forced to.

Inu barks from the back seat and I subconsciously flip the watch on my wrist over, confused. The numbers are too high, but this isn't the time to worry over it. Inu barks again, giving away our position and I naturally brace for the onslaught of bullets as I reach for my gun.

Instead of my gun strapped to my chest, the desperate flailing of my body comes into contact with Inu's wet tongue. I try to push her off but she's insistent, trying to climb over the back of the Humvee.

"I'm pulling over," Smith says from beside me.

He flips on his blinker and turns down the music that had already been playing in the background, a heavy metal song Smith loves to play on repeat. Without the noise, I begin to realize there's something off about the Humvee. About Smith. Inu being here. Me.

As soon as the hazards flick on, Inu is finally able to gain a grip on the car and jumps into my lap, her wet tongue hot and humid against my face.

"Isamu, would you like the med bag?" Gonzales asks, voice steady and even.

I fight for air against Inu's incessant care and rip open the door, throwing my legs over the side of the Mustang and inhaling humid air as deeply as I can. Gonzales's hand is tight against the back of my shirt, and I try to bat him away weakly.

"It's fine," I tell him through a gasp. "I'm good. I figured it out."

But he doesn't let go until a precariously balanced Inu starts kneading against my legs, like a cat making bread.

We don't speak as I listen to the cars drive by, trying to haul my brain back from the desert. My fingers itch for cigarettes I don't smoke anymore, and I supplement it with running my hands through Inu's coarse fur. Her big brown eyes look up at me and I watch her wet nose flare as she smells me. She presses her nose into my chest and stops her kneading.

"Do you need anything?" Gonzales asks, hand warm where it rests on my lower back in silent support.

I'd had a similar incident in the cab ride with my mom as we headed back from the airport in Tokyo. She had laid my head on her lap and ran her fingers through my hair, repeating, "imagine all the cherry blossoms we'll see once we go to Kawazu." I imagined them then and try again now as Inu presses against my aggressively beating heart.

"Can you, uh, can you change the music? This is Smith's favorite song."

Cars are a little rough on my PTSD without the added bonus of the music I listened to while in Afghanistan.

Gonzales changes the song, finding a completely different genre as he puts on some pop hits. I'm forced to put in strength I don't feel to lift my prosthesis and Inu back into the car. My breathing is still shallow, cramped even further as we start driving again.

"You can hold my hand if you want," Gonzales says, voice light in joke even though his words hold concern.

"Suck my dick," I gasp out, craning over Inu to look over at him, taking his hand all the same. It's more for him than me since Inu already grounds me.

Gonzales and I immediately break out into sibling-like bickering that helps ease me into calmness more than anything else could right now. I missed this. I missed Gonzales's sharp humor and bear hugs. I missed his kind heart and easily given smiles.

"I missed you, fuckhead," I tell him in a break of our easily flowing trash talk.

He releases my hand to clasp my shoulder as we take the exit, making sure to mind both the dog still hugging my chest and the curves of the road.

"Missed you too, *güey*."

As we wind down the roads, the dark green giants encroach the car. They're preparing to fall and crush us under mother nature, not even a lick of blue sky visible between their branches. It feels like a fantasy world—with leaves too green to be anything but full of magic, and air rich with the smell of life. North Carolina is an envious landscape with these trees, making even most city slicking folks long for the countryside.

The trees finally expand and branch out as we approach my childhood home. On the farthest end in a suburban neighborhood, it seems to randomly erupt from the surrounding woods.

When I was little, the trees behind our house served as a jungle gym for Gonzales and I. We'd pretend we were on the back of woodland giants as we climbed them, or dive and roll between their trunks like ninjas—stealing their branches and swinging them around like the katanas in my dad's bedtime stories.

As we grew up, we invited our friends from the basketball team as we ran through the trees playing tag, until someone finally thwacked themselves on a branch so hard that he split his forehead open.

We barely visited the woods in high school, instead spending all our time at the basketball court or the gym. The only time I really went back was when Gonzales appeared outside my door in the middle of the night, eyes black and blue, limping visibly as he dumped his and his sister's bags on the floor.

He bowed low to my concerned old man, a sign of respect in our household, and asked if they could both stay with us. That night, Gonzales and I sat out in the woods smoking our first joint as he threw rocks—and eventually punches—at trees.

Gonzales stayed with us even after his sister went back home, mentioning something about apologies and shiny gifts from their mother. All bought with a credit card taken out in Gonzales's name.

At the end of Duke's school year, all those memories will belong to someone else. I hate that my dad is selling our house.

I peek over at Gonzales and watch his eyes trace the memories in those trees.

"When's the last time you came home?" I ask him.

"Last Sunday. Your old man puts up your Ramses stuffie in your seat."

I groan, imagining my ram stuffed animal sitting at the dining table. "He does not." I'm sure he does because even if I was never smart enough to go to the Duke, he supported my lifetime obsession with its biggest rival: UNC. Well, he hoped I'd go to school there, but I knew from the start that college wasn't for me.

Ignoring Gonzales's laughter behind me, I ease the car door open. Inu drops to the grass gracefully, more like a gazelle than a rottweiler, and picks up her foot in offense at the damp grass.

"You don't need me to hold your leash now, right?" I ask Inu.

She shakes her head—more a complaint about the moisture than in response—before I tell her, "Get busy," the general command to let her know she's free to piss at her leisure.

The door to my parents' house swings open, revealing my dad in his typical house slippers and an apron—a survival tool he picked up after my mom was forced to bail on us in order to care for her ailing mother back in Japan.

"You tell me I can't pick you up from the airport but once you're finally here, you don't even come in and let me say hi to my granddaughter?" His arms flap around in tune with his flailing hair leaving numerous strands sticking out left and right. He's clearly been pulling at it as he tries to gather his bearings in the kitchen. It's good to see him making the effort.

I look at Inu where she's crouching and taking a shit in my dad's beautiful green lawn; better than the intricate Japanese Garden he keeps in the backyard. "Inu had to pee," responding to my dad in Japanese, just for the opportunity to call her dog.

My dad frowns at the name and looks down, and I realize he isn't looking at her as his frown deepens. I wore shorts today because it's the easiest way to go through airport security. He's seen my prosthesis before, but I know it still makes him sad.

He turns and clomps back into the house, where I can already smell bamboo and the sea as food cooks, and I give him the space he needs to get his emotions back in order.

"Are you really going to leave? Now that you're finally back, I mean," Gonzales asks.

"Yeah man." *What's the point in staying if no one will be left*, goes unsaid.

The army was my ticket to citizenship. Early retirement and a lifetime paycheck are just added bonuses. The idea of seeing the world has always been more appealing to me than sitting behind a desk at some nine-to-five. Now, I just don't have anywhere to come home to when I need it. My dad will be in Japan and who knows where Gonzales will be.

Gonzales follows my dad inside, taking off his shoes at the door and sliding on his own slippers, comfortable in a house that's as much his as it is mine.

I feel some semblance of relief after my welcome, even though I have to crouch on my swollen thigh to pick up Inu's crap. The discomfort from the car is slowly dragged out of me like a rusty knife being pulled from my gut.

All of my boxes are piled in my dad's living room when I walk in. There are blind spots all over, the forest looming beyond my dad's expansive garden, hiding men holding guns. The knife digs deeper.

I stiffly maneuver around the boxes to the kitchen, grabbing an icepack from the fridge while I dodge my dad and Gonzales cooking dinner. My dad intercepts me as I walk past him a second time and pulls me down to kiss the top of my head. He says something that sounds distant and buzzy to my tinnitus affected ears.

I pat his back, wishing for a better reunion but too fixated on the pain in my thigh and the fears in my head.

Returning to the living room, I haul my med bag and backpack over to the couch before plopping down.

"Inu, closer," I call.

She approaches from where she's been hesitantly watching me, waiting for commands, and I unclip her own medical bag before undoing her support harness.

"Release."

Before I can even offer her a treat for a job well done, she takes off. Her teeth flash as she sprints through the house so excitedly that her back bunches up and her tail whips back and forth to assist her sharp turns. She zooms around the boxes until, tuckered out, she ventures back to me.

She shakes out her fur and I stroke her back as I pull a treat from my pocket to feed her.

"You were such a good girl," I coo quietly as she leans into my scratches, tongue lolling out in satisfaction from her spent energy.

I know she's a service animal, but I've always wanted a dog. This isn't necessarily how I imagined it happening, but the joy is still there. There's a calming presence from having her so nearby. It was once that moments alone quickly turned to fear and terror, nothing but my thoughts to keep me company. Mood swings caused by my PTSD make me bitter, angry, depressed, apathetic. I feared that who I was becoming was a husk of the man that I once was.

But now when I wake with a shout, hands clutching a limb no longer present, it's Inu's wet nose I see; tongue lapping at the tears shed in my sleep. Bitterness has transformed into coarse fur between my fingers; anger, the wagging of a tail; depression, a walk through a sun-soaked park; apathy, a caring mouth to feed and love.

Inu has rekindled my hope that this journey is far from over.

I pet her head one last time and she flops to the ground, huffing out an exhausted breath. It's been a big day for both of us. Tomorrow will be more tiring.

Shifting my prosthesis, minding that I don't hit my poorly deposited backpack or dog harness, I begin the process of taking it off. My residual limb is achy and my nerve endings are firing with pain from the altitude change of flying. I pull my socket until the suction releases, laying it on the ground next to me. Rolling off my silicone liner, my scar-ridden skin is exposed beneath, but I feel nothing but relief as everything in my body suddenly unwinds. Like taking off a tie or a bra after a long day but more intense.

The TV remote is just out of arm's reach—delaying the next best part of my relaxation routine—and I stare at it with longing before hauling myself up and using my single leg to hop over to it.

The highlights of the Panther's game fill the house, accompanying the sounds of my torn-apart family and their torn-apart cooking. Inu quietly snores below me as I massage pain cream into my residual limb. The Panthers are trash this year, and I groan as another pass is intercepted. The TV continues playing as the cream dries and I put on my compression shrink—something I only use on days that cause exceptional swelling. Traveling really is the worst.

Grabbing some decorative pillows, I prop up my leg before adjusting the still cold icepack to ease the swelling. I finally feel the first relaxing breath enter my lungs, chasing away the serrated knife with distraction and peace, and I let myself fall into it as I cart my fingers through Inu's fur.

Chapter Two

John

I'VE WORKED AT MULKEY'S auto shop since before it was legal for me to have a job. That's one of the upsides of a rural small town life. I'd come here straight after school, throw on a too big uniform that blended in with the rest of my too big clothes, and help my dad change oil while he discretely drank from a flask.

Toward the end, it was me changing the oil and fixing suspensions while my dad was laid passed out behind the tires. Even Pops Mulkey couldn't turn a blind eye to what a safety hazard my dad was—army vet or not—but when my dad eventually got fired, I begged to take his job, memories of hunger pains fresh in my mind. Pops was kind enough to employ me under my father's name until I was of legal working age.

It's because of those years of experience that I'm higher staff which means better pay, but, also, dealing with the day-to-day bullshit.

"Love," Tom calls from the front desk. It's not a term of endearment when he says it, just my surname that resulted in playground bullying and a big patch on my oil-stained work uniform that says "LOVE". Everyone else has their first name, but Pops is convinced having my last name on there makes me seem friendlier.

It's more like a cruel joke the world is playing on me. Me, who lost all the love he knew in the world at the early age of ten. Me, who still gets uncomfortable when Aaliyah casually says, "Love you". Me, who is more inclined to believe love is a chemical lapse in judgment than a lifelong commitment.

I slide out from under the Honda I've been working on and calmly make my way over to the front desk. Tom is visibly forcing a placating smile at the woman across from him. Her face is flushed in anger, hair frizzled even in the lower autumn humidity, but what worries me are her clenched fists. We'll have to call the cops if she swings, and that'll mean an early end to my shift and less pay.

I don't stick around for cops.

"How can I help you, ma'am?" I ask, letting my Southern drawl flow like honey in hopes it'll fill the gaping holes in her still cracking façade.

"I came here earlier today for a simple oil change and now they're telling me I need to have the engine repaired." Her squawking voice makes my right ear ring—the side where my dad once shot a gun beside me while he was drunk.

It was a cruel reminder to both of us that no matter how badly he wanted to have well-meaning bonding activities, he was too drunk to ever achieve it.

"Hmm, let me pull up your file and give you the lowdown." I handle the ancient computer with one hand and work out kinks in my lower back with the other, all while keeping a pleasant smile on my face—not too big that it appears sarcastic, but not so small that she thinks I could care less.

I try not to think about how bad my body aches or how often I have to fight to keep my eyes open. Thinking about things like that doesn't make it any easier to get through the day. I work almost every day at the garage—doubles on Saturday and an afternoon stolen on Sunday—then another job on campus, and not to mention my constant studying to maintain the GPA for my miniscule scholarship, while also participating in more extracurriculars than I can handle. All in hopes I'll keep getting internships that might mean something by the time I graduate next year.

This angry Karen is just another dollar in my pocket. The longer and slower I talk, the more time I have before I have to get under a car.

Besides, judging by the Karen's nails and pristine white shoes, she can afford to pay a little of my tuition.

I peer at her incident report and think, maybe not.

"Ma'am, I'm sorry to tell you, but you waited so long for the oil change that..." I take a second to adjust my words into something that will make sense to her. "Well, it clogged up your engine and some parts aren't in working condition."

It's an expensive fix, but if she takes it to the dealership, she'll lose her warranty on the car—a brand new Jeep Wrangler with a yellow matte custom paint job. Judging on the miles it's already accumulated and the state of it, she completely missed the first oil change. It's tens of thousands of dollars that she's thrown down the drain because she couldn't care for her customized Jeep.

It makes my teeth ache with something like jealousy. I push the feeling aside like all the rest. There's no benefit in wondering why folks like her get all the money when I did nothing but work hard for a scrap of it.

"That can't be right," she complains. "Someone like you couldn't possibly understand the intricacies of newer cars like mine. It has to be a programming issue."

I'm exhausted enough to choose to believe that her slight has more to do with blue collar work than me being Black.

"I'd like to speak to your manager."

I stifle my smile and continue to massage my shoulder. "Ma'am," I say slowly, reveling in it. "I am the manager on duty."

I continue to massage my shoulder calmly as she yells at me. Profanities slip from her mouth and tears finally begin to fall when she fesses up that it's technically her daughter's car—a graduation gift. They didn't even have the foresight to check if freshmen could have cars on campus before getting it though.

Oh, to be the privileged few.

Despite my stoic expression and lack of response—I'm more concerned with the knot in my lower back than her supposed sob story—the Karen proceeds to tell me how she wasn't supposed to be driving the car at all and panicked when the oil light came on. I don't even bother nodding, only eyeballing the clock above her shoulder as I watch the time on my shift dwindle more and more.

She's full-on sobbing when the clock hits six.

"We'll have that out for you as soon as we can, but I suggest getting a ride home since it won't be done today, seeing as its closing time."

Or this week, for that matter.

I turn, leaving the woman gasping behind me and grab my stuff from our staff room. "You finish my suspension?" I ask Tom as I toss on a loose button up—it'll have to do until I get back to the dorms to shower off.

"Yeah. She seemed like a bitch."

"Don't use that word," I tell him, already clocking out.

Aaliyah's dorm smells like incense and nail polish. I add the smell of men's body wash into the already weird mix as soon as I step in.

Her roommate—Keelie—gives me a patented awkward white person smile from where she's studying on her bed, bracelets jangling as she gives me a delayed wave.

I nod at her and step closer to Aaliyah's side of the room, where Aaliyah lays splayed on the floor with cardboard and paints surrounding her.

I groan at the itching feeling in my fingers—it's a compulsion at this point—and pull my Polaroid camera from my bag. I snap a picture and sit across from her, the rectangular film flapping between my fingers as familiar a sound as a tab clicking open on a beer can.

"John, you're a guy," Keelie starts.

"As far as I know," I respond, grabbing Aaliyah's notebook beside us, reading off the details about the Rally that Aaliyah has updated this weekend without me.

"What does it mean when a guy says he wants to get to know you more before he asks you out?"

Aaliyah sighs, long and drawn out, forcing a smile to crack my face.

"It means he just wants to sleep with you," I tell her, not beating around the bush. I'm still feeling shitty because of the Karen and the job and the homework and my morning spent in air-conditioned classrooms.

Keelie groans and Aaliyah and I both prepare for her typical onslaught. "Liyah, would you date me?"

Aaliyah snorts and shakes her head. "No chance. You threatened to hit your ex with a car."

Keelie holds up a finger. "Once and it wasn't like I was actually going to do it. I just wanted him to hurt the way I hurt."

I cough into my hand—hiding a laugh. "Maybe you just need to go into it knowing he's a man who can't commit. I always look for men who can't."

"Really?" she asks.

The first guy I hooked up with when I got to Duke was looking for something more. He was a khaki wearing Chinese frat boy two years ahead of me and I thought I'd picked safely. It had been more miserable than standing outside of the food bank when I was a hungry teenager. He wanted to know everything about me, keep me around, and make something out of what I thought was a one-night stand. I didn't give him anything but my body since he'd end up leaving one way or another.

Since then, it's just been quick romps with guys off Grindr, usually in their messy beds or in the back of the car. Those are worse because I'm always worried there's some poor wife at home putting the kids to bed, wondering why her husband is suddenly working so late. But I have needs too. Even if they aren't necessarily emotional.

I finally shrug at Keelie, picking up a pencil so I can start drawing the flyers we're putting up. I'm art-oriented, but when I had looked into prospective careers in the field, it was simply tabled as a hobby.

"I like men. Especially the ones I shouldn't."

Aaliyah laughs and reaches for one of my locs, tugging at the golden hoops fed through them delicately. "Did you ever hook up with that guy at the Fuqua Pride meeting?"

"Oh?" Keelie asks, always thirsty for gossip.

"That meeting dragged on, as expected from a bunch of business majors. But no," I tell Aaliyah with a scoff. "I don't shit where I eat."

Aaliyah frowns and I look away to start my sketch. She means well, I know she does, but there isn't a good way to explain that my biggest fear is opening up to someone enough that would qualify past a one-night stand. I'm afraid she'll send me to grippy sock jail if I show her even a sliver of my soul. I'm even more afraid that I'll guilt her into holding my hand through life as to not be another person who's left me. It's better to keep my fears to myself.

"John—"

"Don't start," I tell her as I finish painting a line of the Duke Chapel, where part of our rally will be.

"It's important to open yourself up to relationships," she starts anyway. "I have literally never even seen you give a guy a second look. Sure, they don't always go well, but you can always learn something from them."

I roll my eyes. "Yeah, you learn a lot from the last girl you dated?"

Aaliyah frowns at this, and Keelie begs an explanation from her.

"On God, she looks at me and says, 'you're not like other Black people.'" Aaliyah sucks her teeth in anger. "She genuinely thought it was a compliment, and I genuinely showed her the door." She glares at me, either annoyed that I brought it up, or annoyed that I'm right and not every relationship leaves you feeling like a better person.

"I'm sorry—" Keelie begins but Aaliyah raises a hand.

"Nuh-uh, don't need your pity when it's my daily struggle. I only wish I'd gotten it on recording so I could've gotten her fired from her job. Now she's out there in the world with her racist beliefs, probably doing racist things." Aaliyah sighs. "Let's move on."

In the corner of my eye, I see Keelie put in her earbuds, sensing the end of a conversation. I reach out and place my hand on Aaliyah's. She squeezes it back and mouths, "love you." At least with each other, we understand the anger and exhaustion that comes from microaggressions and blatant racism.

"I only wish back then I could own my anger," she tells me, now that Keelie can't hear. "Seriously, John. I swear you still code switch more than me."

I flash her my customer service smile, doing everything in my power to not look like a thug–which is code for Black. When I drop it, she gives me a sad look that I return. Aaliyah has often expressed to me that she feels like her life would've been easier if people didn't see her as an angry Black woman at the simplest complaint about mistreatment.

I look away from her and down to the poster, feeling like there is no break from the struggle.

When requesting that the campus put more effort into the fight for Trans Youth—and of course, all Transgender people who face their medical rights being stolen from them–it's probably a moot point. It feels like a moot point. I'm a political science major, and it feels like half of the debates I study now are either trans rights or the more silent, underhanded bills being passed while we worry about LGBTQ+ rights.

North Carolina itself bans gender affirming care for those under eighteen, despite medical research detailing the benefits of it. No puberty blockers. No voice therapy. No affirmation.

There are some students on campus under eighteen. Early achievers who skipped more grades than I even want to think about. What if they'd been looking forward to getting out of their parents' grip to finally start their transition only to be met with these new, bigoted laws?

My hands shake as I attempt another straight line of the chapel. Aaliyah reaches out and cups my hand—a mirror of my earlier comfort.

"Hey, it'll be okay. I'm sure lots of people will show up in support."

No matter how little I've given the rest of the world, Aaliyah has still been able to read me like a book.

I flash her a small smile, because I'm not as strong as Aaliyah. It's better to keep my feelings far from my heart. "You're right. It'll probably be packed," I lie.

In truth, I believe that soon the entire country will follow Missouri's suit and ban gender affirming care for some adults as well. It feels like a repeat of the Black Lives Matter protesting.

A camera will point at us, calling us brave and bold and a changed America. At first, maybe some politicians will budge or they'll throw us a bone or two—performative actions like cops kneeling and taking cops to trial—only to turn around and hit us with tear gas or rehire those fired cops in different districts.

I used to think political science was a major that could help me change the country around me, but the longer I spend looking at the news, the longer I feel like politics are too fucked.

It makes me want to shout, and scream, and burn down a building. But no one would listen and since I have nothing better to do, I continue on with the flyer that will probably end up under band flyers and ads for new roommates. If not for me, then for the trans kids who are too scared to have a voice yet.

My lips press against each other with the desire to say something. Anything. *Do you think this is pointless? Do you think we're actually going to make a change? Do you think one day they'll run people like you and me out of town?* But I don't because I can't.

"Okay, that's *that* sign done," she finally says, fanning her hand over the wet paint. "I'll bring it to the Fuqua Pride meeting on Tuesday. Unless, of course, you want to?"

I shake my head at her and show her how far I am in the flyer.

"Ugh! I'm so jealous. I've always wanted to be able to draw."

"Nah, your sign looks great," I say. "Drawing takes too long anyway. You'd be tearing out your hair by the end of it."

She pulls at a spiral tucked along with the rest of her afro. "I'm thinking of putting in braids."

"Basketball season is coming up and you'll miss blocking everyone's view," I tell her with a grin. I love basketball, I only wish I had been able to play somewhere other than the concrete courts at the end of the trailer park.

She laughs and grips my forearm. "Not if you go with me! Then it's even better because no one says anything about you being tall."

"Well, now that you've got Gonzales, he'll cover the sides too with his shoulders. Seriously, he's huge."

She smirks mischievously.

"Oh God. Stop. I do not need to know the guy's dick size," I complain.

She holds up her hand. "I won't. I won't. Promise. But just know that you're a subpar gay friend for it."

I roll my eyes. "That's homophobic."

"I'm pan," she argues.

"Fine. Gayphobic and stereotyping," I reiterate before holding up my drawing. "Your turn."

I don't like my handwriting, especially if it's going to be displayed.

"Do you ever just take a break?" Aaliyah asks when she looks up from the flyer only to see me already working on assignments. "You're like an Energizer bunny."

"I wish."

Everything I'll need to finish this paper is organized in front of me, and I put my notebook in my lap as I get started on the final few chapters.

"Do you want to borrow my laptop?" she asks.

"Nah, I'll just use mine later." I've written all my papers by hand and I've got a general idea of when I reach my word count this way. Transferring it over isn't too tedious as long as I use a computer at the public library; I never know when mine will randomly shut off from overheating.

"One day, when I'm rich, I'll buy the fanciest computer money can afford. Then, I'll never even turn it on because I'm rich and I can afford it," I tell Aaliyah wistfully, thinking back to the Jeep sitting in the shop.

"If I were rich, I'd fund your campaign to run against my dad," she responds, lying on her stomach beside me.

We sigh and think of all the things we hope the future holds. Even though I've become cynical, it's impossible to tamp out the small fire burning in my heart that longs for things to improve. One day, it'll either grow so bright that it'll obliterate everything, or it'll fizzle out as it's smothered by the world.

Isamu

It feels like I belong on the couch after these past two days and I hate it. I've been missing my leg for long enough that I'm as used to it as I can be, but it's still a blow to my ego when I'm being knocked flat on my ass from moving into Gonzales's apartment.

It doesn't matter how much therapy I've gone through, it's still a shock every time I'm limited by my prosthesis. But I am. No matter how much I train, or work out, or rehab, or get my prosthesis adjusted, it won't ever be the same. The prosthesis isn't some sort of super-powered, high-tech upgrade like it is in the movies. It's a supplement; a tool to help replace what's been lost, but it isn't the same. My residual limb swells inside of the prosthesis and sharp phantom pains still keep me up at night. My other leg aches from overcompensation, spine tight and sore despite the hours of gait training I've put in.

Once, I carried one-hundred and twenty pounds of equipment across the desert, complaints on my tongue. Now, I'm thankful to be able to carry these boxes. Not everyone is so lucky. It took a lot of therapy and time spent wallowing. Even now, I still catch myself resentful on days like today. It's impossible to not feel some sort of resentment as I realize how limited I've become.

But my life from before is gone, filled instead with a new perspective—a new day—that I will never take for granted.

"Son," my dad says, because that's how he speaks. "Son," like we're the imperial family instead of a bunch of immigrants searching for a better life.

"What?" I respond, because that's how I speak. "What," like I'm an immigrant who chose a life with my finger on the trigger instead of being trapped behind a desk. There wasn't ever a winning choice between either capitalistic hellhole.

"We've already put your bed in the room. You can go take a nap and we can get this all finished."

I groan and look over at my dad. Gonzales is sweating from underneath a box labeled *Video Games*. Three flights of stairs are a lot, even for people with two legs.

"Do not worry. I am still strong," my dad supplies with a grin, flexing his lean muscles.

"Speak for yourself, Takeo. I think I've lost twenty pounds." Gonzales sets down the box and wipes his brow.

My dad smacks him across the stomach. "Don't listen to him, Isa. In just a week, he'll regain his healthy coating with all that Pozole he's been making."

I laugh, just imagining my dad trying one of Gonzales's dishes and complaining about the saturation of flavor. Just like when Gonzales first moved in with us.

He may have been a little quiet but in the kitchen, Gonzales always came alive. Something about caring for his also beaten-down sister was healing for him. After she left, Gonzales stayed in that kitchen like it was his own form of therapy. I would loiter around on the countertop until one day, he finally asked me if I'd show him some Japanese recipes. And then it became *our* therapy.

Gonzales has always been there for me like I've been for him. All in and one hundred percent, but I can never ignore an opportunity to pick on him.

"Hey," I start, pointing at Gonzales. "Just because your food tastes so bad you have to cover it up with chili doesn't mean we have to eat it." I smile to let him know I'm only saying it to get him riled up, but riled up he gets.

Boxes in my dad's car are long forgotten in favor of rough-housing. We end up jostling each other, dodging boxes under our feet, and I threaten to call his new girlfriend to come over and wrangle him, even though that's far from the truth.

Inu wags her tail and barks, off duty and anxiously watching the humans around her behaving so strangely. My dad sits down calmly on the couch and turns on whatever show he's been watching, knowing this is going to take a while.

Eventually, after Gonzales has given me a speech about different spices from Mexico while holding me in a headlock, I wander down to my dad's car and grab a box. When I turn around, Inu is sitting patiently beside me.

"What are you doing here, hun? You're off duty." I scratch her behind the ears.

"She is nervous because her dad will not relax. You should listen to me and rest now."

I look up at my old man who has apparently also come to investigate my comings and goings. He walks over and puts his hand around my bicep.

"We have not had a chance to really talk since you came back."

I shrug but give my dad a smile. "I mean, I just came back yesterday."

He nods as if I've told him everything. "How is your mother?"

When my mom left to take care of my grandmother, I was just starting basic training. It was weird to be so enveloped in this world of exhaustion and getting through the next drill, that I don't think I ever gave myself the room to fully understand. It wasn't until I came home and my mother wasn't there that I finally realized things had changed. I never had the heart to ask my dad if it was some sort of separation, but now that I know he's retiring to go live with her, I feel worse than I did back then somehow.

My mom took me all over Japan when I went to visit, but never once did I see my grandmother. Even if she was sick, it's not like there wasn't free health care. But maybe that's callous and selfish. Maybe I just want my parents back the way they used to be before I left—sitting around the dinner table, enjoying each other's company while all doing different things. Chopsticks in hand, I'd be watching film of our next basketball opponent while my dad poured over assignments and my mom read gardening books.

I only wish I'd known it would end. I would've looked up from the screen a little more often.

"Ma's good," I tell him. "She misses you and said she'll be sad to see the garden for the last time when she comes to help you pack."

He smiles and looks away, hopefully lost in a good memory. It may just be my own fears that surround him moving because I know they've been looking forward to being reunited since my mom left. The last time she came back was only because of my return from Afghanistan, sans leg.

"Come, Isamu. Please rest and Gonzales will bring your things up while I make us all dinner," he tells me, using his grip on my arm to herd me up the stairs.

No matter how old I've gotten, my dad always tries to take care of me. It's kind, but obnoxious.

There's only a few boxes left which is the only reason I take him up on the offer, pointing at Gonzales and saying, "since chili is so good for you, I'll let you get the rest.'"

I lay down a box in the pile that takes up half the living room, then get started on my process of care for my residual limb. Gonzales finishes bringing in the boxes just as the smell of katsu fills the kitchen.

I hop over to the bar on one leg, Gonzales poking my sides in an effort to trip me up—opposing hand out to catch me just in case—and sit at one of the stools.

"Why are these so tall?" I complain as I look at my single leg dangling from the stool.

"Have you thought about being less short?" Gonzales asks.

"Jesu—" I cut myself off, realizing my mistake. "Dude, shut the fuck up," I finish lamely.

"Nah, come on. Say it," Gonzales eggs me on.

I roll my eyes as Gonzales sits beside me. My dad stays standing, preferring to eat that way so he can pace, and the plates of breaded chicken laid out before us.

We all quickly open the meal by saying the Japanese words. Even Gonzales says it—saying he prefers it over the Catholic prayer of his childhood.

"No. I can't believe I forgot." I lift a piece of chicken between my chopsticks and rub it into the Tonkatsu sauce pooled on the plate. "When I got to the military, everyone thought I was religious because I always hesitated before saying it."

"Saying what?" Gonzales asks, playing dumb.

"What did you tell them?" my dad asks.

"Told them I was living with a self-absorbed—Jesus Christ!" I shout, being cut off from my sentence as Gonzales sticks his wet finger into my ear.

"You called?" Gonzales asks, finally pleased I've said his first name.

"Stay pure for Jesus," I add, out of habit, even if I'm annoyed that he got me to use his first name.

"I feel like it shouldn't even count if we say it like Gee-zus instead of Heh-seuss," I complain, lapping at a bit of chicken stuck to the corner of my mouth that I almost spit out when Gonzales harassed me.

It falls and I reach for it, and Gonzales's hands come out to make sure I don't fall from the stool. He sees me stick it in my mouth and grimaces. I shrug, not one to waste any food after too many MREs.

Being surrounded by my family—including Inu—fills me with a sense of rightness. There were times when I was afraid I wouldn't get this again; when I was scared it would never be the same. But right now, with katsu warming our bellies and laughter in our throats, I feel like nothing has changed. At least, not yet.

Chapter Three

Isamu

INU CLEARLY NEEDS TO pee. Which would be a non-issue if I had my prosthesis on, but the fine dusting of sleep still lingers on my eyes, and my residual limb lays comfortably over the blankets I kicked off last night.

I groan and roll over in bed, only slightly wishing I could cover my head with a pillow and pretend she doesn't have any needs. I get out of bed, reaching for my crutches that pull uncomfortably at the hair in my armpits. Gonzales's neighbors—my new neighbors—are in for a surprise if they haven't left for classes yet.

"Settle," I tell her as I heave my way to the door in nothing but boxers.

She follows me, minding the crutches as we slowly make our way down the stairs.

"Get busy," I mumble out, rubbing sleep from my eyes.

The sun hasn't even finished its morning climb but here I am, giving the neighbors a peep show. At least I'm still in shape. Physical therapy was depressing until we finally learned how to squat with the prosthesis. That's when I really started feeling like myself again.

Now that I'm back to mobile independence, there's only one way to celebrate. Nothing speaks true freedom like hitting the road without a care in the world. I'll really be putting this leg to the test when I hike up every 14'er in the US, and down every canyon and crevice Inu and I can fit into. National Parks, State Parks, just a cute little trail on the side of the road. Whatever it is, Inu and I are hiking it.

But before we can even do that, I have to convert a camper van so it can fit a full-grown man, a ninety-pound rottweiler, and an entire living space for the both of us. It's going to take a lot of research and I'm not sure how much it'll cost me, but I've got until spring to figure it out.

I pause my train of thought as Inu finishes her business, and I frown at the shit that she's left behind. I didn't think to bring a poop bag.

Looking around to check for neighbors, I turn and leave the shit steaming in the early morning air. It's not like they're going to yell at a half-naked disabled man. Probably.

The apartment is spotless except for the stack of broken-down cardboard boxes by the front door. Even then, there are still small touches of Gonzales everywhere. A few mementos from our post-graduation trip to Mexico I barely remember—including a tequila barrel just slightly larger than my palm. One of those stuffed army bears that Gonzales made when he went with my parents to drop me off at basic—my last name, Miura, is sewed into the pocket of the bear's Army fatigues. And more textbooks than I can count, stacked haphazardly on his bookshelf.

Nerd.

Grabbing Inu's food bowl, I spy a mug from Atlanta. I didn't even know Gonzales had been there.

I hold the mug in my hands, thinking of everything I've missed out on. This was supposed to be our lives together.

There's no point in regretting it now, but I allow myself to wallow once I'm standing in the shower, one hand tightly wrapped around the support bar as I lower myself onto the stool, a few tears dropping. Looking down at my residual limb, I try to staunch my bleeding thoughts before finally accepting their release.

I lean my head against the shower wall and let the water wash my tears away. Finally, Inu's nose pops through the shower curtain, probably making sure I'm still alive in here.

"Hey, pretty girl," I say, voice as wet as the air trapped in the bathroom. I run a pruned hand under her jaw and she sniffs, trying to gauge my heart rate under the smell of my clean skin.

The vice grip that sorrow had around my heart is alleviated by the tears.

Inu watches me get out of the shower, patient and calm as water droplets fall inches from her snout. She has to back out awkwardly, allowing me the space to crutch out of the bathroom naked. I mimic the beep reversing trucks make as she takes tentative steps backward through the now open bathroom door.

A door in the apartment squeaks open and Inu and I both pause, still as we wait in anticipation.

"Did you know Gonzales was still home?" I ask Inu in a stage whisper. She huffs at me.

I'd assumed he'd have started classes earlier than this.

"Oh my—I'm so sorry! I—I'm late," shouts a woman I've never seen before, averting her eyes, then looking back in confusion.

I blink at her in surprise but make no move to cover myself as she finally looks away. Privacy wasn't exactly something I got in the military.

She scurries across the apartment, heels clacking against tile as she snags a backpack hidden behind all the boxes.

"Aaliyah," Gonzales starts, carrying a T-shirt in his hands as he leaves his room. "Wait, I can drive—what the fuck? *Oralé*, let me get some of that," he jeers before slapping me in the dick with his shirt.

"Seriously?" I groan, crutches keeping me from folding into myself for protection and comfort.

I can't believe I cried for this asshole in the shower.

He chases after the girl who's already left the scene of the crime.

"Would you rather take the bus? I can drive," Gonzales yells from the stairwell down at the girl.

I don't wait to hear her response and rush to my room, slamming the door shut once Inu and I are safe from Gonzales's harassing hands.

I put my head in my hands before finally picking myself and my virtue up off the bed.

Slipping the silicon liner around my residual limb, I redirect my thoughts to the long day ahead.

"We did a lot of research on vans last night, huh?" I tell Inu. "It's going to be expensive even with the military disability check." Turns out losing your leg to falling rubble kind of sets you for life. "But we might have to get a job if parts start to get expensive."

I push the air out of my liner and attach my prosthesis.

Last night, I tried to come up with a list of functions I needed for the van and almost instantly became overwhelmed. Some vans have video gaming systems, others have bathtubs with jets. Even the most basic builds were too overwhelming to try and understand all the components that went into it. That's when the YouTube walkthroughs of van conversions were helpful, and a familiar auto shop appeared in one of the fancier builds—Mulkey's.

"It's been a while since I've been there," I tell Inu, stepping into my leg to evacuate the air through the top. I was forced to take a day off from wearing it because of the aches. "I'll let you in on a secret, girl. I have no clue what I'm doing."

My hobbies were playing basketball and cooking meals with

Gonzales, not working with wood or taking cars apart.

I strap Inu into her harness and am surprised to find Gonzales still in the apartment, humming happily as he stands in front of the stove. Smells like bacon.

"What'd you think? She's gorgeous, isn't she? And get this *güey*, she's a double E major," he says, smirking over his shoulder before dropping a plate of bacon in front of me.

"What's double E?" I ask.

"Electrical Engineering," he clarifies with a waggle of his eyebrows. "She's perfect, a genius, and *mierda*, she's a badass."

The thing about Gonzales is that he could sweeten a nun into bed. I attach the leash to Inu's harness while I casually say, "Too bad you're gonna lose her then. I bet it must be difficult for your girlfriend to realize she's dating the guy with the smaller dick."

Gonzales scoffs, pauses in thought, then scoffs again. "Shut up."

"Whatever," I tell him, slipping a piece of bacon into my mouth before shoving on my boots. "We could compare but—" I suck my teeth hard. "That'd be pretty gay."

"Ha! Yeah, cause you'd never do anything gay," Gonzales jokes, where he's begun picking off the plate.

I flip him the bird while slipping out the door with Inu.

"Do you want a ride?" he shouts from inside.

"Nope," I respond, grateful for the exercise after a day of rest. Last night, when I was researching how to convert a camper van, I found companies that do it for a hefty price. But I want to learn how to do it myself, since I don't know how long I'll be using it. If any repairs are needed, I better be equipped enough to do it on the road.

In high school, I drove a used mom van that broke down at least twice a year. Mulkey's was just off the highway, past the trailer park, and easy to get to between school and home. I just didn't realize they would also do custom builds for vans.

By the time the bus drops of me and Inu about half a mile from the actual auto shop, I'm regretting not taking Gonzales's offer for a ride. The sun is high in the sky, cooking Inu's dark fur and my darker hair equally.

If only North Carolina understood it was fall.

"Let's get your booties on," I tell Inu, crouching down to unzip her little carrier bag and pulling out her dog shoes. The pavement isn't too hot for her paws, but the sidewalk is nonexistent this far in the sticks, and I don't want to risk glass or worse as we walk through the tall grass.

She drinks from the portable dog bowl I've set out while I strap her into her shoes. The prospect of a van seems sweeter now that I'm violently reminded how miserable travel is in the US.

Mulkey's is surprisingly busy for a weekday morning, judging on the number of people in the waiting room. There is a guy manning the counter, old sweat splitting apart the grease coating on his face. His beard is scraggly and his hair comes out in tufts underneath his ballcap.

"What can I do for ya, sir?" he asks as I reach the counter.

"Hi," I start, violently remembering my southern accent that's never sat right on my tongue. "I actually saw your shop on a Sprinter van conversion, and was wondering if that's something y'all offer."

The guy smiles, slow and rueful as if he's remembering an inside joke. "Mhm, yeah, I know the videos you're talking about. But nah, we don't offer anything like that. It's just one of the guys, he took some extra money to work it." The man pauses. "Definitely regretted it though," he mumbles under his breath.

"Well, does he still work here?"

Grease man nods and turns around, opening the door to the garage and releasing the sounds of machine and sweaty car mechanics in the process. "Yo! Love! Come here."

I don't see anyone look up but someone from inside shouts, "Love's in class," as another yells, "He's working on the Corolla, you need him?"

"Yeah! Some guy's here about a van conversion," grease man shouts with laughter in his voice.

Finally, he shuts the door but two seconds later, another man emerges. His uniform says "LOVE" in big letters but there's none in his eyes as he glares at grease man, eyes shouting displeasure his face doesn't betray. Wiping off his hands on an oil-soaked rag, Love's eyes snap to me and he blinks his long lashes once, slow, like he's trying to will me away.

"What can I do for you, sir?" he asks, bracing his muscle knit arms on the counter to lean closer.

It makes me feel like I'm in a cage with a bear. It makes me feel intimidated. It makes me feel excited.

"Did you do the van conversion on YouTube?" I ask, letting my accent drop as I focus on not letting my voice crack. Attractive men make me weak in the knees—knee I suppose—and the tingle of anxiety crawls across my skin.

He nods slowly and I wonder if he's intentionally trying to make me feel like the scum on his grease rag. My attraction diminishes. "Yeah, but that's the only one I'm doin'. Ain't got time for no more."

Grease man walks away, laughing to himself from behind his fist. Love's eyes follow him with annoyance.

"I'm Isamu." I hold out my hand to him, which jostles Inu a bit.

He ignores my hand and looks down at her, jaw tightening. "She bite?"

"No. She's a service dog. I'm disabled." I immediately panic that it sounds like I'm pulling the pity card instead of just trying to avoid getting kicked out and move on quickly. "I don't need you to do the conversion for me. I just have a lot of questions and I was hoping to ask someone who has experience in it."

"I'm kind of busy here, man. I don't think—"

"You don't have to answer them now," I rush to cut in. "You're at work, I get that. What if I emailed you some questions?"

He raises an eyebrow and rolls out his neck, the golden hoops in his locs shining in the store's awful fluorescent lighting. "I'm sure there are some companies who'd answer your questions, or one of those social media influencers that live in those vans."

"I'll pay you. Just for the questions."

He folds his hands over each other on the counter and rests his chin on them, plump lips puffing out in thought.

"Leave your number and I'll think about it. But I'm real busy man, so don't hold your breath."

I nod vigorously, writing down my number quickly, excited to not feel so lost on my project. "Thanks so much, Love. I seriously appreciate it," I tell him.

"John. Name's John."

I look up from where I'm writing and grimace. "Sorry, I thought with the—" I point at my own shirt. "Okay, well thanks John," I finish, sliding my number toward him before turning to leave.

As I look back to make sure Inu gets through the door without trouble, I watch him toss my number in the garbage bin before returning to the garage.

John

Aaliyah's boyfriend is in my garage this morning, driving a flashy white Camaro with electric blue racing stripes. Apparently, he asked for me specifically, which caused Tom upfront to crack a joke that I need to stop inviting my boyfriends to work. He won't be laughing when I crack one of his ribs.

"Hey, what's up, man?" Gonzales starts, clasping his hand in mine. Normally, we make the owners wait in the front, but Tom thought it'd be funny to tell Gonzales he can go into the garage to greet me.

"Working," I say, lifting the hood of his car. I wish I hated this car, but it's a working model of the 1969 Camaro my dad and I have sitting outside the mobile. It's from the year before health and safety rules were enforced. Before engine powers were lowered and other regulations were added, such as smog pumps and power steering. I'm screaming with jealousy that his car is up and running.

If I had the money, mine would be purring stronger than his.

My dad would still be salivating if he were looking at this car.

Tom and I start the basic check, seeing if there's anything other than the basic oil change that needs to be fixed.

"This is a nice gig you've got here," Gonzales says after a long period of silence. "Being able to move around before an entire day in class must be nice."

I'm a quiet guy. It goes with the territory of having a dad who never listens and a mom who never can again. Because of my silence, I've learned to listen to others. I can tell when someone is building up to say something that I'm not going to like.

This is one of those times.

I'm not merciful enough to cut to the chase and give Gonzales an out because sometimes, people will still bail at the last second despite all their build up. I'm hoping he bails because if he's about to ask me what to get Aaliyah for her next birthday, he'll be disappointed to learn she's more likely to enjoy going to a Black poetry reading, versus a shiny new piece of jewelry he can just throw his Camaro money at.

"I actually have a favor to ask."

"What's up?" I ask him, taking a reluctant pause from calling out checks to Tom.

Today is finally cooler, and the humid North Carolina summer slowly begins to release in its delayed realization that it's autumn, but my shirt still clings to my back and chest. I look over at Gonzales and run the rag across the back of my neck, annoyed that I'm still waiting.

"That guy that came in yesterday for the van conversion—"

I scoff and begin to change his oil, already uninterested in talking about the guy, no matter how nice his ass looked in those Lululemon pants I've never been able to afford. The last van conversion I worked wasn't worth the money. The customer was a pain, constantly changing his mind after I'd finished part of it and cracking constant jokes about all the ecstasy trips he'd take in the van during music festivals. It made my skin crawl knowing he was another addict in my life.

"John," Gonzales starts again, sounding too calm for my heat-stroked nerves.

Aaliyah really knows how to pick them, but thinking of her makes me feel guilty. I hold out a hand to Tom to hang on. Leaning against the car like the asshole I am, I cross my arms as I face Gonzales, giving him my full attention.

"What?"

Gonzales's eyes drop to my arms and back to my face before he smiles. I thought I was good at putting on a placating mask for customers, but Gonzales is on a level I didn't know existed.

"That guy, Isamu—"

"Isamu," I agree, reminding myself of his name.

"Yeah, well, he's my roommate and he's really looking forward to converting that van. You see, he just got out of the military—"

I grunt, uncomfortable with military sob stories when I've been living the residual of one my entire life. Still, knowing that's the reason why Gonzales is here, it tugs at my heart strings more than I'd like to admit. I know how hard it can be to watch someone you love come back as a different person.

"And it's just his dream to have one and travel across the country with his dog."

"His service animal?" I ask, gritting my teeth at the thought of already being lied to.

"Yeah, Inu. Isamu has a transfemoral amputation." Gonzales places his hand on his thigh, his eyes bright in a false sense of calm.

I fight the urge to turn away, rolling out my shoulder instead to rid myself of the excess energy. "I don't have the time, man."

"Listen, Isa will pay you just to help, and I can take some of the load off your plate so that you'll have more time. What's got you so busy?" Gonzales asks, placing his hand on my shoulder.

I'm a big guy. Taller than Gonzales, but less muscular. It's not often that people try to touch me, and I can't help but stare at his hand in confusion. He removes it.

Gonzales couldn't do my homework, and it's not like I'd even want him to. Judging by his car being here, I doubt he'd know the first thing about cars, except maybe how to change a tire. There's no way I'd trust him with the secret of my father's care, and I've put in too much work for the trans rally to pawn that off onto someone else.

I wrack my brain for a way to get out of this, filtering through every conversation I've had with Aaliyah until I find the right piece of information.

"Fine," I agree, turning back to the Camaro I'd much rather be dealing with. "I'll help your buddy. Under one condition," I tell him, turning to press an oil-stained finger against his chest. "If you can beat me in a game of one-on-one, I'll help him build it. If I win, give me the Camaro."

It's the most outlandish condition I can think of, which leaves me pleased. I know he'll decline them, and I can continue on with my day.

Except Gonzales says, "Alright, deal," with so much confidence that either this guy has a million Camaros in his garage, or he should be on the Duke basketball team.

I nod, hiding my surprise and hand him his keys. "Your car's done."

In small towns, word travels fast. In small campuses, word travels faster.

"Did you challenge Gonzales to a pickup game?" Aaliyah asks when I sit beside her in gender studies class, recently showered clean from the garage muck.

I grunt an affirmation as I pull out my laptop—not one of the expensive ones Duke's IT suggests, but a cheap version I found second-hand. Aaliyah sets her touch-screen laptop next to mine, covered in various stickers from college clubs, abortion rights, and pansexual flags. My own laptop is scratched but I don't use stickers to cover them up. Half of them are mine anyway from trying to fix it so often.

"He played all through high school and he still plays like every week," she says, speaking above the sound of my loudly whirring laptop.

If it weren't for the online portion of the class, I wouldn't take it out. Everyone's used to the loud groaning machine by now but at first, it gained too many curious looks, and I wanted to dig into my skin and bury myself underneath it.

"I'm better," I tell her confidently, looking up at the professor as she begins her lecture.

"So, what? You're just going to take his car instead of helping

Isamu with the van?" Aaliyah throws off her coat, not seeing when I cringe at my own shitty situation.

"Yep."

Every semester, I put more on my plate than I can handle with no end in sight. Summer isn't even a reprieve because of the unpaid internships at some campaign office or new age think tank, followed by late nights working at a fast-food joint on the edge of town, in hopes no one from the office will see me.

Last summer, I couldn't even afford an apartment in DC. I slept in my car and paid for a gym membership just to shower in the morning. All the money I had made from converting the last van went into my tuition or my dad's medical bills.

The van was a pain of a conversion. It was for some coked-up rich kid who decided he wanted to be a social media influencer instead of a lawyer like his dad. His father supported it financially, as long as the kid kept quiet about his father's affair. But of course the rich kid told me all about it. And about how a fixture for the solar panels was unnecessary when duct tape could do the job, and about how he wanted a marble finish on his counters—after I had already stained the wooden counter that would be in his kitchen.

I wish he would've just thrown his money at it and let me work in peace.

"John, is everything okay? I get you're a cranky old man, but you're normally not this bad," Aaliyah says.

"How long would you say it took me to do the last conversion?" I ask her quietly, simultaneously taking notes and filling out some forms on my laptop. It feels like I'm always doing five things at once.

If only I could just breathe.

"He said he just wanted to ask questions, not for you to do the whole conversion," Aaliyah counters.

I raise an eyebrow at her because we both know how it'll turn out. There's a lot about remodeling that people don't understand until they're staring at it in the face.

"Six months," she finally says.

I wave my hand as if saying, *see?*

"I accidentally saw his dick," she whispers. "Isamu, the roommate," she adds at my confused look.

I drop my pencil and turn away, a grin wobbling on my lips.

"Already tired of Gonzales's?" I ask, teasingly.

Aaliyah grabs my shoulder, turning me back toward her just so I can see her glare.

"Come on, you know it's all about the motion of the ocean," I tease.

She rolls her eyes but can't help the laugh that escapes her. "It was an accident. Did you know he has . . . I don't know the right way to say it—"

"Say it the wrong way then."

"He's missing... parts? Gonzales says he has—"

"An amputation," I correct, forgetting Gonzales's exact words this morning.

She pulls her coat back on, the AC getting to her as the sweat from walking across campus freezes. I look back at the professor and catch up on notes.

"So, roommate's dick. It's a prosthesis?" It's only half a joke because now that the idea is in my head, I wonder if that's why Gonzales was so interested in the rally.

"No. It's uh, from birth—"

"A growth, if I may," I supply, eyes still on my notes so I can stuff away my grin.

Aaliyah is starting to blush under her dark skin and if I continue to egg her on, I may actually let a laugh slip.

"That's gross. You may not. No, just shut up. Let me explain. He was coming out of the shower as I was leaving for class—"

I look up in shock. "You're sleeping over at his place?"

She gives me a deadpan look. "I said let me finish, John. Also, yes."

I don't have to tell her that sleeping over at a guy's house with another large roommate sounds like a bad idea. She can see the thought on my face. Some people would call it paranoia, but those of us on the receiving end of dicks call it safety.

"Anyway," she continues when she sees I'm staying silent. "He's coming out of the bathroom, but he doesn't have a towel on. He's just all," she gestures between her legs. "Free. Probably because he had crutches and was missing his entire leg."

"Hey, if it's big enough, then at least he's got another."

I avoid the glare she sends me by taking notes, biting the grin on my face.

"You are such a man. I swear."

"Thanks," I tell her, drawing a penis on her touchpad with my finger.

"Oh, fuck off," she giggles as the professor looks up and glares at us.

We both duck our heads quickly and get to work after that.

Chapter Four

Isamu

I WATCH THE SLICE OF pork slip from my fingers, meeting the floor with a wet slap. Inu doesn't so much as flinch from where she lays beside me. Service animal or not, she deserves her fun. Her ritual zoomies after work leave her sleepy.

"Release," I tell her. She was already released since we got home from the gym, but she still doesn't move. "Eat." I try and she moves forward to sniff it.

"Maybe she just doesn't like it—oh, never mind." Gonzales stops himself as she gobbles it up, watching from across the kitchen island as he drinks his pre-workout.

"Such a good girl," he coos at her, then looks at me. "What are the meal preps for? You actually going to start leaving the apartment? Get a job?"

"I've left every day this week, dickbag," I complain, popping a pea into my mouth. It does little to satisfy.

"Pics or it didn't happen."

Gonzales claps his hands loudly just as I'm gearing up to snark back at him. My heart rate automatically jumps at the snapping sound and Inu huddles closer to me. I scratch her behind the ear and feed her an actual training treat. This is precisely why I'm not supposed to give her food off the ground and mistrain her—she could miss a cue if we're too busy mucking about.

"Alright, children. I'm off," he says. "I have a one-on-one game tonight."

"With who?" I ask, rubbing my chest. My prosthesis wasn't made for endurance sports like basketball—it isn't responsive enough. It's ridiculous that insurance companies don't consider sports prosthetic limbs "medically necessary", leaving me floundering for other options. There's a non-profit organization I've already reached out to in search of a sports-specific one for hiking.

"Aaliyah's friend," Gonzales says, suddenly reluctant to make eye contact. "John Love."

I look up from my kitchen drawer rifling. "Auto shop John? Tall, handsome, and rude as all hell, John?"

Gonzales looks at me with interest and I lose the battle against my blush. When I had told Gonzales about the mechanic who threw out my number, I didn't realize they knew each other.

"Everyone is tall to you, Isa," Gonzales says.

"I just didn't know you guys were pickup game buddies," I say, ignoring the barb. It's not that far off.

"Eh. Well, he's Aaliyah's best friend." Gonzales frowns. "Just trying to keep on their good side."

I sit up, finally noticing the lack of eye contact, the hands fidgeting against his keys, the things going left unsaid.

"What aren't you telling me?" I ask. I haven't truly had a chance to meet Aaliyah, but if   she's the type to force her boyfriend to do things he doesn't want to, even something as small as deal with her unkind friends, our meeting will be anything but pleasant.

"I may have made an agreement with him that if I beat him, he'll work on the van for you."

I suck in a breath. Looks like I'm the asshole forcing my friend to fight my battles for me.

"It was a shitty thing to do behind your back, but it just got out of hand," Gonzales says with a shrug. "Truthfully, I thought if I just asked him, he'd help you out."

I groan, annoyed that now I seem like a needy, clueless fuck. Which I am. But John didn't need to know the full extent of it.

"And he agreed if you could beat him in a game of one-on-one?" Gonzales sucks his teeth.

"Alright. Let's go watch you win then," I tell him, quickly pulling my greens off the stove and shoving them into storage containers for the week.

Gonzales shuts off the stove as I pull on my shoes.

"What's in it for him?" I ask as we pile into the Mustang.

"Eh," he says. "We don't need to worry about it because I'll win."

If John played around here in high school, I don't remember him, and I remember almost everyone. It was my job as our point guard to know the competition and learn their abilities. Basketball used to be everything to me—my entire personality. I used to think it would solve all my problems, but no matter my skill, I was too short to play anywhere past high school.

John's already at the court when we arrive, perfect form as he shoots basket after basket into the hoop. Aaliyah sits in the grass by the pavement court and waves at me awkwardly.

I wave back feigning nonchalance, but regardless, my cheeks heat up with delayed embarrassment.

"Dude, you might lose," I tell Gonzales, watching John's thigh muscles flex as he dribbles the ball easily behind his back and makes a break for a layup.

Gonzales doesn't reply and goes straight to John, but I'm forced to sit beside Aaliyah as I pray against hope that she won't bring up my dick.

"You're not going to play?" she asks, reaching out to pet Inu.

"Don't pet her," I tell Aaliyah. "She's on duty." It always makes me feel cruel when I tell people they can't pet her, especially kids, but if she misses my elevated heart rate in a moment of distraction, worse things could happen than just hurt feelings.

"Oh. My bad."

I wave her off. "I can't play with this prosthesis. I'd need a straight blade if I really wanted to, but most of us play wheelchair basketball."

She hums in thought and says nothing else, so I turn to the guys warming up. Gonzales is defending John, but I watch as John's calves tense and can see the fake coming that Gonzales can't. John breezes past him easily, not even needing to use his shoulder to gain space.

"Your boyfriend is going to lose," I tell Aaliyah.

She laughs. "I sure hope not."

"Not cheering for your best friend?" I ask, knowing Gonzales would be rooting for me to lose if the tables were turned. Only because he's grown tired of watching me be the best.

When I was at the helm, we went undefeated all four seasons in our conference. Gonzales played JV until junior year, when he moved up to varsity with me.

"Eh," she responds.

"Did you ever play basketball?" I ask Aaliyah as the guys continue to warm-up.

Aaliyah laughs but it sounds barbed; angry and resentful. "Nah.

My dad thought basketball was a sport for men and butch lesbians. Jokes on him though, volleyball didn't make me any straighter."

I look over at Gonzales, stretching his arm after missing a shot—as if his were the problem. "Yeah, I can see how Gonzales's bubble butt would fulfill that need."

She snorts, surprised, and covers her mouth with a well-manicured hand.

"Tell your dad that basketball doesn't make hetero men either. Or, at least, it didn't in my case."

"Oh?" she asks.

I think there are little whales painted on her nails, but I can't tell from this distance.

"Don't worry, Gonzales isn't my type."

He's definitely bit off more than he can chew. It's obvious as soon as the game starts, when John easily pushes off of him to make a three pointer.

"Speaking of him," she starts with a conniving smile. "He told me to never call him by his first name, but he won't tell me his middle name."

I match her sly grin, sensing revenge.

"Maria," I tell her, just as Gonzales trips over himself trying to rip the ball from John on a rebound. John offers a hand to help him up and I can't help but notice his arms, glistening with sweat. "But there's a nickname in Hispanic Culture that people named Jesus Maria go by. You'll have to ask him for that one."

I'm not so eager for revenge that I would give Aaliyah his childhood nickname. He says just the sound of it throws him back into the crap his mother put him through. It's his choice on how much he wants to tell his girlfriend about it.

"So, you don't have a nickname for him or anything?"

I tear my eyes from John. It's an effort.

He's amazing. Despite his size, he hardly uses force to break away from Gonzales; instead, relying on speed. John's good enough that he could have easily played at a lower division college.

"Nope. Gonzales. Full thing." He has a million nicknames for me though: *culero*; *pollito*; *güey* and, of course, plain old Isa.

By the end of the game, I'm enamored with the way John plays, and I quickly leave Inu and Aaliyah behind. I should be distraught that Gonzales lost by a landslide, but I can't find the emotions underneath my awe.

"Holy shit, dude. Where did you play? I would've definitely remembered you if we ever played against you," I ask John, grabbing his forearm. My hand slips against his sweaty skin.

He wipes his mouth with the bottom of his shirt and my eyes drift toward his exposed skin. He isn't cut, instead just a soft layer of stomach, making his speed all the more impressive.

"I never played except for on the streets," he admits easily as Gonzales walks off to his car.

"You're joking," I say. "But you're amazing."

He doesn't smile or say anything, but everything within me itches to try again.

"Why didn't you play in high school, if you don't mind me asking?"

Before John can answer, Gonzales slips past me and thrusts out his hand. "Bets a bet," he says, placing the keys to his Mustang and a sheet of paper in John's hand.

John pants, still tired from the game, and looks down at the paper: the title of Gonzales's car.

"Wait, what?" I ask, shocked and confused.

"John, you can't be serious?" Aaliyah stomps over to us, hand offering a water bottle despite the annoyance on her face.

John takes a long drink, his throat glistening in the setting sun. He looks at me, and I realize I've been staring.

Averting my eyes, I look at the title of the car, not having realized the trade-off of the bet.

"Your friend must really care about you," John says, only speaking to me as if no one else were around. "I'll help you with the van conversion," he says, pushing the title and keys into Gonzales's chest. "Not just questions. You and I both know you need more than that, but you're paying me for my time, and I can only work after class if I don't have any club meetings and never on Sundays. Deal?" he adds, holding out his hand.

"Deal," I tell him, grasping his hand.

Inu barks behind us. John's hand flinches in mine but his face doesn't so much as budge.

John

The Poli Sci textbook in my backseat looks at me angrily. I glare back, just as annoyed.

"I don't know if I told you how proud of you I was. That was considerate of you the other day," Aaliyah says from the passenger seat.

"What was?"

I know what she means, but the last thing I want to do is confront the unshakeable feelings from my childhood. I couldn't help but think of my dad each time I scored a point on Gonzales. Maybe if someone had helped him once he came back from deployment, my life would've been different.

I take a turn onto the small streets of downtown Durham.

"Agreeing to help out Isamu even though Gonzales lost."

I snort. "Yeah. He lost bad, huh."

Aaliyah flicks me with a chipped nail. There's whales on it because she's on a "Save the Whales" kick. I think sometimes it's easier for her to care about animals than humans; it's too exhausting dealing with racism in every part of society. "Don't be a sore winner. You'll start sounding like my sister."

Soft rain falls down the windshield and I keep my eyes glued to the road, even though the vulnerability in Aaliyah's voice begs me to look at her.

"Sorry. I didn't mean to," I tell her regretfully as we take a sharp turn. "Have you talked to her at all?"

She laughs sarcastically. "What? And listen to her say I'm just following the 'woke agenda'? She's always in line. Never a hair out of place in dad's perfect campaign family."

I bite my tongue, giving Aaliyah the space she'll no doubt need to rant.

"I mean, she's my big sister. She should have my back." Aaliyah traces a falling droplet on the front window of my car with a sharp nail. "What if they find out I'm dating Gonzales? Then they'll start saying it was all a phase. Sometimes I think I did engineering because it is as far removed from a Stay-at-Home mom that I could find."

I park in the only spot I can find that doesn't require me to align mirrors and reverse, then turn to Aaliyah.

"Liyah, shut up." I grab her shoulder. "Last week, you brought me a circuit board you built that moves a mechanical arm thing for surgery. Do you remember that?"

She nods, mouth still pouty.

"I'm not going to lie and say I understood any of it. But you were, and are, so damn proud when you make one of those little Arduino things—"

"Arduinos are for middle schoolers, John," she says through a sniffle.

"See? I definitely know seniors who still program their circuit boards with Arduinos, and you were doing that shit in middle school. You love this stuff. Don't let your parents tell you programming a Ubisoft thing isn't cool."

She laughs. "It's Ubuntu, and it's a Linux software."

"Please stop," I beg her. "Or I may actually learn something nerdy." I squeeze her shoulder and she surges forward, wrapping her arms around me.

I cradle her against my chest. "Just remember when you're making more than your sister by making electrical things go zap, she's probably changing her umpteenth million diaper of the day."

She snorts against my chest before slapping me on the arm. "There's nothing wrong with being a stay-at-home parent," she says, keeping me in check.

"No. Of course not," I agree. "Unless it's your sister."

Aaliyah sighs and unravels herself from me. "I guess we better get in there. The guys are probably waiting for us." She wipes underneath her eyes, careful of her makeup, and jumps out of the car.

The air has quickly cooled down and I reach into the car for my worn Duke zip-up. It strains against my arms, still fitting my eighteen-year-old body and not getting the memo that I've gained some weight and muscle since then.

McCabe's is relatively empty when we come in. Aaliyah and I would normally go to the on-campus bar, but I think Gonzales is trying to show how grown he is by taking us off campus. I follow Aaliyah as she weaves us to a booth where the guys are sitting. Isamu's sitting by one of the shelves built beside the booth, laughing at one of the books. The dog is seated below the table, but as Aaliyah slides in beside Gonzales, I'm forced to sit beside it. I tuck my legs in as close to my body and as far from it as I can manage.

"Hey, man." Isamu puts away the book, happier to see me than his dog is.

I nod back and realize I relate more to the dog's serious demeanor than its over-excited owner.

"The drink menu is one of those phone scanners if you want a beer," he tells me as I pull off my jacket.

"He doesn't drink," Gonzales answers.

I'm surprised he picked up on that from a single afternoon at his apartment.

I've never told Aaliyah why I don't drink. She's never asked, and I've never offered anything up she didn't need to know. It's one of those things that makes our friendship so easy. Aaliyah doesn't pry at the boarded-up closet I hide, and I don't gawk at the skeletons in hers that she so easily shows me.

"I'd give anything to be able to drink like I used to," Isamu complains, resting the hand not clutched to a stein glass on his thigh.

A group of loud guys walk into the bar. Isamu's eyes flick over to them and back, shoulders tensing. It reminds me of my dad, and I can't help but wonder how long Isamu has been back from deployment.

The dog gets up suddenly and I flinch away, my right butt cheek suddenly off the booth seat as I try to squirm away from it. It ignores me, nosing at Isamu's leg instead, but Isamu is staring at me instead of the dog.

"So, midterms are coming up pretty quickly, huh?" Aaliyah says loudly as she attempts to divert the attention away from me.

Gonzales clears his throat and leans forward. "Yeah, I feel like I don't know how I'll find more hours in the day to study and write all my papers."

"She doesn't bite." Isamu says quietly.

I grunt, which to me says everything, and to everyone else says nothing.

"No. Seriously," Isamu starts again in a whisper as the other two talk around us. "Service animals have to go through years of training, and they can't even get out of their puppy training if they have bad behaviors like biting or obsession with food."

At my silence, Isamu lets it go and easily flows back into the conversation, proudly boasting that he doesn't have midterms to worry about.

"Maybe you could help me study for my addiction and substance abuse midterm?" Gonzales asks Aaliyah, his mouth downturned in a pout.

This time, I don't let my body show my discomfort.

Isamu laughs, cutting in before Aaliyah can answer. "Yeah, because you guys got a lot of studying done the last time she came over?"

Aaliyah glares at him, only to receive a flash of Isamu's bright pink tongue in return.

"*Culero*," Gonzales complains.

Isamu only shrugs and takes a sip of his beer.

One of the loud guys from earlier slaps a table and Isamu's glass slips from his grip. I quickly reach out and grab it, just barely keeping it from tipping all the way, but beer still drips down my hand. The dog barks. I fight the urge to pick my feet up.

"Does anyone want another round?" Isamu asks, staring blankly down at his half-spilled beer.

Gonzales and Aaliyah don't even get a chance to respond before Isamu is crowding me in a silent plea to get out.

"I'll give you a hand," I tell him, standing quickly. But when Isamu follows me and slides out of the booth, he beelines for the exit with the dog in tow, walking tight circles around its owner.

I look back at the table. Aaliyah looks just as confused as I am, her eyes widened in surprise. Her hesitation has Gonzales locked into the booth and I make a split-second decision. Did my dad have a moment at a bar when no one reached out to make sure he was okay?

Gritting my teeth against my own behavior, feeling the weakness of my bleeding heart, I follow Isamu out of the bar.

The air nips at my skin, prickling it in goosebumps as I realize I left my coat inside, but Isamu is slowly falling against the fence surrounding the outdoor seating of McCabe's.

"Can I sit with you?" I ask, staring at the dog who is pressed against his lap.

"Just don't report to Gonzales," Isamu answers. His knobby fingers aggressively spin a silver cigarette case.

I sit beside him.

"I quit after deployment," he explains, holding up the empty case. "Bad habits die hard though."

"How long have you been back from deployment?" I ask, resting the back of my head against the fencing.

"Two years. Afghanistan. Why don't you like dogs?" he asks, inhaling through his teeth in longing for a cigarette. I watch the curve of his neck as he blows out harshly. It's a mirror of my dad's own addiction, but Isamu's fingers are still empty.

"How'd you lose your leg?" I counter.

He smiles and lifts his pant leg, showing off the metal. "IED blew up one of the patrols, outside of the building my team was checking. Building fell on my leg."

I nod, feeling guilty that the question came from a place of anger. Isamu should have shoved the question in my face but he doesn't, and I leave that information for much later. "I grew up in a trailer park where the dogs were purposefully starved to make them angrier. Every morning, I'd walk to the school bus with the sounds of their chains snapping behind me. I was afraid one day, one of those rusty chains would break and a dog would tear into my neck."

The dog's eyes are still fixed on her owner, but I can tell by the flick of her ear that she can feel my gaze.

"Rottweilers like her."

"She won't bite, and she most definitely isn't starved," Isamu says, patting her belly softly.

"I'm sure," I lie. "Don't tell Aaliyah I told you that."

Isamu's fingers begin to roll a phantom cigarette. His tongue darts out to lick his lips as he hums in thought. I think of finding a sleazy, depressing Grindr date after this.

"Why?" Isamu asks, and I startle away from the sharp curves of his jaw. For each of his hard angles, I have a soft one.

"She'll be sad I've never told her any of that."

"Why'd you tell me then?"

I huff out a breath, looking into the street where cars are parked, shiny from the sprinkling of rain that fell earlier. I can't tell him it's part of my masochist streak to shoulder everything alone, but there is another truth I can say.

"You know that 'Stranger on a Bus' thing?" I ask.

He raises his eyebrow and looks at me more calmly than anyone who's sat here having a conversation with an asshole has any right to look. If the roles were reversed, I wouldn't grant myself the same kindness.

"You're leaving after the van is done, right?"

He nods.

"I can tell you anything because in a few months, I'll never see you again. Anything I tell you will just disappear once you hop in the camper van. There are no repercussions. We're just pit stops in each other's lives."

He looks down and rubs his hand over his dog's back.

"That's really fucking sad, man." He pulls down his jeans over his leg, maneuvering over the dog to do so. "It makes me feel like all of this is a pit stop in life."

"Isn't it? Isn't that why you're leaving to travel?"

Isamu turns the little metal case this way and that.

"No," he says before sighing. "I almost died, or, at least, thought I was going to die. I joined the army because the thought of wasting my life behind a desk is... well, it's just not an option. And it's not like I wanted to rely on employers for a work visa—I needed my citizenship. Now I'm back and everything has changed: my leg, my family. I figured—I *thought* it might just be better if I change with it."

I don't say anything, watching as he begins rolling another phantom cigarette just for the sake of it. It's a practiced habit that his fingers pantomime with the memories of constant repetition.

The dog snuffles and leaves his lap to lay in neutral territory. I scoot away. Isamu watches it all.

"I don't think I have a response for your pit stop idea," he finally says. "But, I'm not unhappy. I'm just... in one of those Eat, Pray, Love stages of my life."

I grunt because I don't understand, but I came out here to make sure he was okay and I'm pretty sure I've done a terrible job of it. I'm not sure at what stage I went from caring about my dad to hating him for his addiction. It's obvious I've somehow projected that onto this conversation.

"My dad always says, 'feelings are a cough that can't be hidden'. Or actually, maybe it's love." He runs a palm over his stubble. "No, he says feelings, but I think it's supposed to be love."

"Maybe you're just not trying hard enough to keep them hidden," I tell him. "But I'll keep that in mind." I won't. "I have class most days after noon and, obviously, work before that. Around seven p.m., I normally work at the athletic center manning the counter or meet up with Aaliyah to work on club stuff. Does four to seven work for your van project?"

Isamu makes a choking sound and looks over at me with wide eyes. "Christ man, when do you have time to take a dump?"

"I save it for the kink show I work after the athletic center."

Isamu's face puckers in an effort to contain his laughter. "First off, fuck you. Secondly, fuck that for actually being funny. Thirdly, don't think I'm not noticing the aggressive change of subject. But I'll let you get away with it this time."

He laughs and leans against the railing behind us. His laugh is something that tugs at me—begs me to take a second look. I turn away.

"Your humor is fucked. If I didn't know any better, I'd guess you served," Isamu says.

"Uh, my dad," I tell him, hoping he won't ask for more. There's been enough deep, meaningful talk to last me the rest of my life.

Isamu looks back at me, his black eyes reflecting the streetlights around us as he searches my face. Whatever he finds there must answer his unspoken questions, because he turns away and stuffs his empty cigarette case into his pocket.

"Well, I won't force you to talk to your pit stop buddy any longer." He grabs hold of the metal bars we've been resting against and hoists himself up. "Besides, I need to find the cutest animated show to watch until I fall asleep." He dusts off the back of his jeans. "See you tomorrow?"

"See you tomorrow," I tell him.

Isamu walks off, and I sit and watch as he and Inu weave their way through downtown Durham.

Chapter Five

Isamu

I MAY HAVE A SLIGHTLY societally-manifested fetish for men who are good with cars. I've come to this conclusion as I watch John swing under a van with ease—his t-shirt riding above his waist and a little bit of his happy trail flashes—I know it isn't the bite of the North Carolina autumn that's blooming goose bumps across my body.

It's not like I'm blind. John's hot. Like, big and powerful with a side of gorgeous and hunky. But I'm kind of romantic and John is kind of an emotionally constipated, straight, asshole. But I can still appreciate the eye candy.

"Gunnar, I really don't know if that's worth it with the milage," he says, muffled from under the vehicle.

Gunnar, the car salesman, who John apparently knows from before his university days, just groans. "John, I'm not cutting you a deal. Go ask Davis, his boss isn't a tool."

"His vans are also shittier. That's why the deals are better." John slides out from under the car. "I'd have to replace an entire engine just to get out of those pieces of shit off the lot."

John and Gunnar have a stare down before Gunnar finally throws his hands up in the air.

"It's my commission, John."

"Yeah? You got a lot of folks 'round here looking to buy Sprinter vans?" John asks sarcastically, his southern twang coming out more to match Gunnar's. "This town isn't as hippie as the college students make it seem. Ain't no one buying these things for anything but cooking meth in their backyard. At least you know he's actually good for it," John says, gesturing at me.

I wave and smile for lack of anything better to sell myself with. I hope Inu is sitting pretty and not sniffing her butthole. Not that she would ever; she's better behaved than I am while she's on duty.

"Fine. All cash and I can give you two percent off."

"The suspension system is covered in oil from a leak, and it's rusted enough that I'll have to replace it," John counters before turning to the engine again. He's looked at it three times already.

"Four percent," Gunnar says, walking forward with a stuttering gait, panicking as John grabs something and shakes it hard.

"How's the alternator?"

"Fine!"

"Really? Belts pretty loose. Sure you didn't repair it at the Jiffy Lube instead of with Mulkey's?" John asks.

This time, Gunnar fully stomps like a toddler throwing a tantrum. He types furiously on his tablet before turning to me and slapping it against my chest. "Six percent. Cash. Take it and get the fuck out. Make sure you take that shit head with you."

John flashes a victorious grin from behind Gunnar. "Don't forget the military discount."

Gunnar sighs and takes back the tablet.

John nods at me and I sign the paperwork there and then under the early morning sun.

"Stay here," Gunnar shouts at John as he leads me inside to pay. Inu's nails click against the vinyl flooring as soon as we enter the air-conditioned building. "You picked one hell of a car guy to help you out."

"Yeah?" I ask as I hand over Gunnar's payment.

"As far as I know, he basically ran Mulkey's—that auto repair shop— since he could hold a wrench. His old man used to work there 'til he got sacked, but John stayed. Shy kid; don't think I ever even heard him talk. Didn't expect him to come marching in demanding a discount."

I hum in acknowledgement and bid Gunnar goodbye. John has every door open on my new van when Inu and I get back outside.

"I've still got the electrical schematics Aaliyah designed from the last time I did one of these, but if you want less or more, we'll have to talk to her again," he says when he sees me approach. "I can't be trusted to design any wiring, but I can do all the rest: strip it, wire what's designed, build and paint the interior. Do you know what kind of style you're going for?" he asks, looking back at me.

He's taller than me and I have to look up to see his honeyed gaze that instantly hardens. John quickly breaks the contact and begins to shut the doors.

"I saw someone put a gaming system in theirs," I tell him. "But don't you need to change the suspension first?"

He smirks and looks down at his watch. "Nope, that was a bluff. If you're looking for a gaming system, you'll definitely need to talk to Aaliyah. She'll have to completely redesign the electrical schematics." John wears his watch on the inside of his wrist. "I'm actually supposed to be headed into the shop for my first shift. I can't meet tomorrow, but I'll come by Monday and strip the van after class. That work?"

"Yeah." That gives me enough time to binge watch videos on YouTube so I don't come off as a total idiot. I don't think I've ever even used a power tool.

"Hey, I figure this is a dumb question, but I feel like maybe you wouldn't say anything unless I asked. You're good to drive, right?" John asks.

I look down at Inu in confusion and then at my prosthesis, hidden behind a pair of green joggers. "Oh," I start, before remembering the John from last night. The one who makes crude jokes and I kind of wanted to be friends with. "Dude, just because I'm Asian doesn't mean I can't drive."

John easily takes the bait. "Could've fooled me, but I guess it isn't just Marines that eat crayons."

I really want to prove myself to John by saying something snarky back, but I'm a one-trick pony—something that Gonzales often reminds me of when he roasts me—so I let out a shocked bark of laughter instead. John looks away, rubbing the back of his neck, but he can't hide his smirk as he realizes he's hit his mark.

After deployment, my buddies came to visit me. We went out to the bars and I watched them try to pick up girls—I'm not out to them for military self-preservation. It turns out our dark humor scared most of the girls off. By the end of the night, most of them were biting it back to combat their dry spell.

I don't know exactly what's going through John's brain as he shakes his head but personally, I'm realizing that I've made a civvy friend other than Gonzales that can not only understand my jokes but play along tenfold.

"You're not too bad, Johnny boy," I tell him. "I'll see you later, man."

I watch him shake his head again, bemused, before walking back towards his car. His jeans flex tightly over his thighs.

Inu pants beside me and I look away from John. The van is where I need to hone in my focus.

Aaliyah meets me in the visitor parking lot beside the Duke Chapel. As I stare up the backside of the building, she eyes my new van.

My fingers itch for the cigarettes I smoked in Afghanistan as I see the building I was so often forced to visit for the annual Handel's Messiah concert. My old man can be such a nerd and I still feel the stiffness of the suit I'd have to stuff myself into just to hear some students perform a dead guy's music.

"Did John go with you?" she asks.

I pull my eyes away from the stone building and watch her run a hand against the side.

"Yeah. He picked it," I tell her, rubbing Inu's neck. She'll be excited to just laze around Aaliyah's dorm for the rest of the day.

I nod and Aaliyah waves me over to follow her. The dorm buildings look like the rest of the campus—stone blocks stacked to make it look like a medieval palace. If I let my mind wander, I can almost imagine knights running around instead of students, townspeople crowding the town square, and some old-time priest ringing the bell high in the chapel.

Instead, there's just students milling about, going from class to class, sitting on the oversized benches as they soak up the autumn sun.

"My roommate is here today too. Hopefully she doesn't give you any problems." Aaliyah opens the main door for me, and I stand inside awkwardly as I wait for her to show me the way.

"Does she normally give people problems?" I ask.

"She's a little boy crazy. She was all over John when they first met."

Laughing, I imagine his dismissive behavior and stoic face must be hard for anyone to flirt with. Although, it also does give him that mysterious vibe.

"Hey Keelie. This is Isamu and that's Inu," Aaliyah says as we step in.

Aaliyah's dorm is covered in, well, everything. It looks like a storm swept through, tossing clothes on top of notebooks and makeup on top of circuit boards. The posters don't look any better, half falling off the walls where they were almost replaced by notes, spared only by distraction.

"He's so cute!" Keelie says, already standing from where she was headed out.

I immediately thrust my leg in front of Inu as Keelie jumps forward, her beaded shawl tinkling in her rush.

"Inu's on duty," I tell Keelie, looking down at where she's crouched in an attempt to get to Inu.

"Seriously?" she whines. "You can't bring a puppo into my dorm and expect me not to pet him."

I bite my lips shut between gritted teeth. I've had a few problems here and there with Inu when I get on the bus or walk into the grocery store, but it doesn't get easier.

"Keelie. Don't be disrespectful," Aaliyah chastises sternly.

"You're right," Keelie starts, brow furrowed. "I'm sorry, new friend, and new friend puppo." She stands up abruptly and takes a step back before extending a closed fist. "I'm Keelie. Nice to meet you."

I knock my fist against hers. "Isamu. Likewise."

But I'm glad to see her walk out the door.

"Anyways... van?" Aaliyah does a clean sweep with her arm across the desk, and a bunch of notebooks and other things tumble to the ground. When she sees the look on my face, she waves nonchalantly. "I'll organize them later."

"Hey, don't let me dictate how you live your life," I tell her with a chuckle.

Watching Aaliyah work is like watching a magician pull a rabbit out of thin air. I tell her the parts I'll need in the van: lighting, a stove, solar panels—and she builds an intricate map of lines and squiggles that seem more confusing than the DC metro line.

It takes longer than I expected because it turns out we need to pick out the lighting and other electronics while we're at it; something about voltage and amperage overloads. Between John's knowledge of cars and Aaliyah's knowledge of whatever black magic this is, I've never felt so inadequate in my life.

While she builds and tweaks the diagram displayed on her laptop, I go through a list of things I'm good at. Basketball, being a dog dad, shooting a gun, cooking—definitely cooking. She emails the diagram to me and John. I'm not sure why she even bothered sending it to me since I can't understand it, but at least she declares step one complete.

"What's step two?" I ask her as she distractedly pulls out her phone.

"I have to put some components together, but you don't need to be there for that." She puts her phone away and looks at me seriously. "So, Isamu. What's your life story?"

I laugh and reach for Inu's thick fur below me. Since Keelie left earlier, I felt safe enough to take her off duty and she's happily chewing on a tennis ball. "Uh, I grew up in Durham. My dad actually works here—"

"He does? What's your last name?"

"Miura," I tell her, worried that she may have had my dad for a class. I've been told by Gonzales that he's kind of a hard ass.

"Professor Takeo Miura is your dad?"

I grimace. "Is that bad?"

She shrugs. "John's had him a few times but I never have. John's a poli-sci major."

"Oh? I didn't even know his major." I feel kind of bad for talking about John when he's not here. He's clearly a private person and I want to respect that. Even if it's unlikely I'll ever get any information out of him.

"Ha, yeah. That sounds like John," Aaliyah says wistfully.

I wonder what their relationship is like when John is keeping his personal life so separate from his best friend. It's a little like Gonzales not telling me about suing his mom because he was embarrassed. Is John embarrassed about his life or is it something else?

Aaliyah and I end up lying on the floor. I trade innocent but embarrassing stories about Gonzales in exchange for brownies. It makes me feel like a dog, especially when Inu ditches her tennis ball to stare at us. She jealously gives us a side eye, knowing she can't beg, but wanting to anyway.

I learn Aaliyah hates her sister. She learns I'm an only child and my mom lives across the world, even though my parents aren't divorced.

"I kind of wish my parents were divorced," she says as she holds her hand above her face.

"It used to feel like my parents were," I respond. Now, it feels like they're divorcing me. "Why do you wish your parents were divorced?"

She shrugs and shifts the pile of clothes under her head. "Then it'd only be one person complaining about my existence instead of both of them. It's exhausting."

I rub my fingers together, itching for a cigarette as I think of how Aaliyah longed for her parents' ferocity to be separated, and I long for mine to be together again. Maybe if Aaliyah had parents like mine.

"Eh, I'm sure they wouldn't even understand that diagram you just drew. It'd probably impress them."

She laughs quietly. "It wouldn't. But it fucking should."

John

A dog chain rattles from the trailer behind me and the back of my neck explodes in goosebumps as I sit on the Camaro, my dad's bottle of gin clutched in my hand. He's sitting on the front steps of the mobile—sober—and watching me carefully.

The air is filled with the crunching of leaves and the conversations inside the other homes, but not with our own voices. My dad runs a hand over his buzzed hair and lets his head fall against his knees.

"How's school?" he finally asks.

I press the closed cap of the gin bottle against my lips. It'd be so easy to be like him; never worrying about anything but when's the next bottle. The gin bottle is warm against my hands but I know if I took a good swig from it, it'd fill my stomach cold as it heavily rested on top of my morals.

"Fine," I snap out, wishing he would just go away. It was going fine, until I checked my exam results online and realized my GPA is going to drop again. Before I knew it, I was sitting out here with the bottle of gin I didn't even bother to throw out when I found it, ass planted on my dad and I's wasted dreams.

"Is it... is it, uh, boy troubles?"

My dad's been sober since I went to college and he got a DUI within my first week away. He still didn't have a job back then, and his military disability checks weren't going to be enough to pay bail *and* the fine. I'd been so pissed off that it took him a week to finally fess up and tell me he'd gotten diagnosed with liver cirrhosis and in his bullshit mind, a drive would help him miraculously come across a new, life-saving liver.

My dad's going to die before I reach thirty. Before he reaches fifty. He's going to leave me alone all over again.

There's nothing I hate more than the fact that it took that for him to sober up. Not me, his own child, fending for ways to feed myself at ten years old. Not him losing his job at the mechanics. He couldn't even be bothered to be sober on any of mom's birthdays or the anniversaries of her death. Only his impending death—only his life—has ever mattered.

But the worst part is that he isn't even a half bad dad, now that he's sober.

I just wish he'd been sober sooner.

"Not boy troubles," I tell him, clutching the gin bottle so tightly that I wish it would just go ahead and shatter against my skin.

Logically, I understand that my GPA dropping a little isn't a big deal. I'm trying to cling onto that thought as hard as I can, using all the tools the free on-campus therapy has provided. But I can't fight the lung crushing fear that in the end, I'll wind up here.

Living in this trailer park, dog snapping their chains behind me, holding a bottle of gin, slowly turning into my father.

I'm just expediting the process.

"Do you wanna—"

My dad's cut off as I let out a scream, frustration bubbling to the edge, forcing its way out of my throat in a tearing sensation as emotion overwhelms me. The bottle neck fits easily in my palm as I bring it down onto the Camaro, letting the scream light the fuse of all my fears and burn them easily all in one.

The broken bits of glass hang off the end of the bottleneck, and I stare down at it through blurry eyes as my pa gingerly takes it from my hand, then wraps his thin arms around me.

"I know, kid. I know." He rubs his hands, already marked with sunspots that he shouldn't have at such a young age, across my back. "It's okay, Jay. Let it out, I've got you now. That's it."

I want to push him away. I want to tell him the reason everything is so fucked up is because of him. Because he took one look at the empty mobile without the presence of my golden, unstoppable mother, and quit. He left me alone to die. I've been dying ever since.

"Jay, let's go inside. I think you cut your hand." He wraps his hand around my wrist and leads me into the house, his other hand wrapping his knit cardigan tighter over his swollen gut. "Come on, boy. Come here. I've got some medical supplies in here," he says, leading me to the single bathroom in the house.

I blink through the tears and look at the dingy mirror, trying to set my facial expression back to neutral.

Back to safety.

"I like your hair. That girl do it for you?" he asks as he pulls my hand closely to his face to inspect it for glass. He clicks his tweezers together—a mechanic looking for a faulty part. But no mechanic can open my heart and fix the loose wires.

"Aaliyah. Yeah, she did."

"Looks good," he says, pouring rubbing alcohol over the cuts.

The worst one is in the middle of my palm.

"I wanted dreads when I was—stop fidgeting, I know it hurts—when I was younger. Your momma said it'd make me look like a hippie."

"Like a Rasta?"

"Like Bob Marley. You know in those Vietnam movies they always play that—what song is that? John, what song do they play when they're flying in the Hueys in those Vietnam movies?" my pa asks.

"Fortunate Son," I tell him, grabbing the gauze with my good hand and passing it over. I hadn't meant to cut myself. Hell, I hadn't even meant to smash the bottle. I'm embarrassed now as I look down at the mess I've made. Normally, it's me doing this type of thing for my dad.

"Yeah. But, did you know, that song came out just before Bob Marley's first album with—"

"With the Wailers. Yeah, pa, I know. Mom hated when you'd put on that record."

He grins, his uneven teeth flashing up at me. "She did. She hated it. Says we should be teaching you blues—music from our people. But I never complained when she'd play you jazz and, boy, did she play you jazz."

"It was her favorite," I agree clinically, pushing away the memories.

"Named you in honor of it after all," he says awkwardly. He secures that bandage and squeezes my hand, causing me to flinch at the pain. "Imagine how ticked off she'd be if she ever found out that me and the guys would let you listen to rap with us. Anyway, the point is, Bob Marley is never played in those Vietnam movies, even though his music was released before the end of the Vietnam war."

"Pa, you didn't even go to Vietnam." He wasn't alive for it. But he was at enlistment age when the towers dropped.

"I know that, boy. I was just talking because I didn't know if you'd gone into shock or something and . . . well, that's what they tell us to do, when someone goes into shock."

"Talk them to death?" I ask, a wobbly grin on my face as I wipe my wet cheeks with the back of my hand.

He squeezes my shoulder. "Do you want to talk about it?"

I shake my head at him and go to the kitchen; focusing on tasks is my sure-fire way of leaving emotion on the backburner. Since it's Sunday, I've been in here meal prepping my dad's entire week. It's hard to see all the meals that went uneaten last week, but at least I can eat them now.

"Dinner," I tell him, slapping the Tupperware container on the coffee table.

The dog barks from the storage unit at the sound of my work boots crunching on leaves. One of the leaves takes a bonus hit as I take a step backward, nervous to get any closer to the dog. Isamu looks up at my frightened face from where he's been staring at a pack of drill bits, like he's trying to uncover the secrets of the universe.

"It's just part of her training to alert me when people are coming," he says before motioning to a wooden container on the workbench.

I continue to watch the dog who has calmly gone back to laying on the hard concrete, despite the dog bed beside her. Feeling as safe as if I were sticking my fingers into a Copperhead hole but itching for the paycheck Isamu and I agreed on, I forge ahead to the wooden box Isamu motioned at.

Only the top is wooden, and I finagle the elastic strap holding it together to open the stack of two.

"Is..." There's food in the box and I stare down at it, not sure what I'm intended to do with it. There isn't a microwave in the storage unit and, even if there was, I'm not sure I want to heat up Isamu's dinner and establish this as routine.

I'm here to work on the van and get paid. Not play housemaid.

"I just kind of figured you didn't have enough time to eat between everything going on. It's a bento box. In Japan, we make them for, uh, friends."

I look back at Isamu, surprised, before looking back at the box in my hand. There are chopsticks attached to the top of the box but not forks.

"Oh. Thanks," I tell him, plucking off the chopsticks. They're nice, not like the kind they automatically give you at the Chinese restaurant in town, which smells like sweet and sour sauce.

I stare at the chopsticks in my hand, debating if I can just stab at the food. I haven't actually had time to eat anything, other than a bag of chips between classes and a cereal bar before my shift. My stomach hurts so bad that it feels like it's either going to start eating its own lining or open a black hole from the pressure alone.

Isamu finally gives up on the drill bits as he sees me clutching the chopsticks in my fist.

"Sorry, I probably should've brought a fork. Here." He holds out his hand and I pass him the chopsticks, watching raptly as he tucks one against the fleshy part of his thumb and the other between the top of his thumb and pointer finger.

"And then you just squeeze," he says, handing them back.

They're awkward in my too-large hand, especially with the gauze wrapped around it. I fumble them a few times, ignoring the smirk on Isamu's face.

"Should I feed you?" he asks teasingly, motioning at my injured hand.

"You should shut the fuck up," I respond, finally grasping a piece of crispy chicken.

I move my face close to the box and take a bite. There's a sauce on the chicken that I've never tasted before, and it explodes on my tongue as the crispy outer skin mixes in with the tenderness of the chicken.

"This is actually really good," I tell him when I finally pause for air—I'm half shoveling, half inhaling the food into my mouth.

Isamu blushes and runs a hand across his stubble. "Thanks, it's karaage. Just wait until you try the dessert. I've always felt like I'm better at those."

I open the box below and eye the sugar-cube-looking object.

"How's the stripping going?" I ask, motioning at the clearly untouched van.

When Isamu looks away, I stuff the sugar cube in my mouth with my fingers and am shocked when my teeth sink into a jelly-like substance that manages to be sweet and savory at the same time. I eat another.

"I unscrewed everything and then the sides still didn't come off, so I went and took Inu to the park, and made food and now we're here."

I stuff another jelly in my mouth and lick my fingers clean. "Did you make sure you got the screws under the caps?"

He nods and I go to his toolbox, full of shiny new toys, and grab the flathead.

"There are latches between the top panels you'll need to undo, and then everything should come apart. I'll show you the first one."

I hop into the van and Isamu follows. As I reach up to undo the first latch, I realize that Isamu is a lot shorter than me. Even on his tiptoes, he may not be able to reach these.

"Can you reach them?" I ask, passing over the flathead.

"Don't be a dick," he responds, his hand warm against mine, a grin on his face. He stretches himself as far as possible to reach the roof.

Subconsciously, I put out my arms to help balance him, but I put them back against my sides just as quickly, afraid that he may take it as an insult.

"You'll stab yourself if you do it that way," I tell him, grabbing the flathead from his hand.

"Is that what happened to your hand?" Isamu asks.

"Something like that." I pop off the other latches—it'll go quicker if I just do it myself.

"When I was a kid, there was this cute little box turtle on the side of the road outside of my high school. It was April, you know how rainy it gets in North Carolina during April," Isamu says, leaning against the van panel's latch. "I thought I'd do the good Samaritan thing and I picked him up to put him on the other side, far into the grass so he wouldn't get hit by a car."

"Makes sense," I exhale as I pry off the panel.

He rushes forward to give me a hand and we carry the panel to the side of the storage unit.

"Right? But, when I turned around to go back to the road, my knee didn't come with me, slipping in the wet grass," he says, gripping his prosthesis underneath his fancy joggers—lilac this time—with the memories of the pain. "Turns out I tore my ACL."

I wince and he smiles, thankful for the shared sympathy.

"It was after my freshman basketball season, so it wasn't the end of the world or anything, but I told everyone I got the injury playing a pick-up game, because I didn't want to fess up and say it was because I tripped saving a turtle."

"Didn't want anyone to see the softy inside?" I joke but I can't imagine Isamu being anything but a blunt, open book he's been so far.

"Not all of us can be as emotionally vulnerable as you," he shoots back with a grin. "Guess the surgery was pointless anyway, since I lost the knee eventually," he adds, softly. "How'd you hurt your hand?"

I freeze from where I'm prying off the last panel from the roof.

"Is this how it's gonna be then?" I ask. "You tell me a secret; I tell you mine? Then you drive away to disappear into the forest with all my secrets, and I stay here holding all of yours?"

He shrugs. "Nope. I tell you a secret and you have the option of telling me a secret, since now you know something that I don't want anyone to know, but you can always not tell me something."

I hand him the last panel, putting the screwdriver between my teeth as I tie my hair up and out of my face, minding the jewelry doesn't press too tightly against my head. "I only meant that as a one-time thing 'cause I felt bad for you being stupid enough to stand under a falling building."

That earns me a smirk.

"But tell me something bigger then, because this is bigger than a turtle beating you up," I play along.

Isamu frowns in thought and pauses to rub at Inu's coarse fur.

"So not embarrassing?"

"Not that type of embarrassing," I correct. "More like, emotionally taxing."

Isamu hums in thought, his bright lips disappearing into his mouth as he chews on them. "Oh! I've got something. It isn't embarrassing, I just never get the chance to tell anyone." He pauses, taking a great breath, a smile on his face. "I'm gay."

I think the concept of gaydar is funny. As if I, along with every other queer person on the planet, should just know when they're in the presence of another queer person. That's of course, not true. If it were, men wouldn't have been wearing bandanas in their back pockets since the Gold Rush, or the 1970s—depends on who you ask. A secret code just to be able to pick each other out in a crowd of straight men.

It may be a trend we need to bring back because my gaydar is obviously nonexistent.

"Why can't you tell anyone?" I ask.

"Well, it's more like I was too scared to. I realized it my freshman year of high school, before the homecoming dance and, well, I didn't want to ask any of the girls. I wanted to ask one of the football players—always liked them big and rugged," he laughs, eyes lost in a memory. "But basketball tryouts were coming up and I didn't want to blow my chances at making the team. Then I just... kept not telling anyone because suddenly I was on varsity, and there was a lot of pressure.

"It's ironic that I was brave enough—or stupid depending how you look at it—to enlist, but not brave enough to come out to my squad. The same secret I'd kept for so long just sitting in my gut, year after year." Isamu looks up at me, gauging my reaction.

My reaction that probably won't be sympathetic enough. I've never known what to say in any situation and this one isn't any easier.

"You've never told anyone?" I ask.

That's a heavy secret to carry just because the timing was never right.

He shrugs. "I got a little brave on deployment, you know, when no one could actually reject me to my face and death was looming at every corner. I sent a letter to my parents and another to Gonzales. Turns out my parents kind of had an inkling when I didn't date anyone in high school. Gonzales just straight up knew because I got so wasted in Mexico that I made out with a guy." Isamu lets out a self-deprecating laugh and motions at me with his hand.

"Your turn. Only if you want to, of course."

I sigh and sit down on the lip of the van. Isamu sits beside me and for a second, I'm scared he'll put a comforting hand on my shoulder.

But he doesn't.

Because we're just pit stops in each other's lives. That's what makes it easier.

I tell him about the exam. I tell him about the bottle of gin. I tell him I'm scared I'm going to turn into my dad. I don't tell him that sometimes I kind of want to, but I can tell he knows.

I don't tell him about the cirrhosis because I don't want to cry.

Chapter Six

John

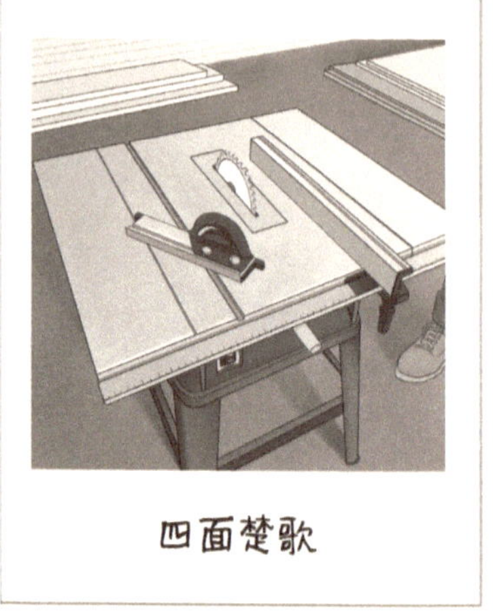

四面楚歌

AALIYAH IS PASSED OUT in her bed when I come in after class, a sweaty mess in my haste to arrive on time. I look at her new set of braids that she likely spent all night finishing, then turn back around. She deserves the rest, and I can handle going to a meeting on my own. Even if it means hiding my exhaustion to appear friendly.

Practicing my smile, I weave my way through campus. It's a good thing Aaliyah lent me her laptop this morning. I don't trust my own laptop to even turn on, let alone project onto a screen. This is an important meeting, and I can't mess up just because of a faulty computer. It's the last club we need to convince to participate in the rally.

A finals week Trans Rights Rally; a big ask but a big display.

It'll disrupt finals, I remind myself. They'll have to listen to us if they're forced to walk across campus through a crowd. It's what Aaliyah has been preaching at every meeting, including the one we had to have with student affairs to get it approved. Given, she tried her best to downplay it, making it seem less like a disruption and more along the lines of, "This matters so much to us that we're willing to lose study time for it."

I clear my throat and squeeze my eyes shut—dreading an environment where I'm the center of attention—before finally pushing open the door. When I enter, the members of the LGBTQ+ club in the law school all look up at me, and I let my smile slide forth.

My handshake is firm, and my speaking voice more so as I go through the presentation. I'd almost forgotten how easily I slip on this mask, just as easily as I slip out of others, but I haven't earned a bunch of political internships for nothing.

"John, your proposal is great, but can't we do it next semester? Or even before finals? It's not that it isn't important, it's just such a stressful time with exams."

The club member's words sting. The hours of late nights planning this—only for her to dismiss it—it makes me bitter. I smile softly at the student speaking; she doesn't realize this is a practiced smile I've seen on all my Intern Directors before they make the most scathing comment about my summer work. It's the look I see on Aaliyah almost every day, and I cling onto her strength if even for a moment.

"Of course," I start. "If the timing isn't convenient for you to support transgender folks as they face constant discrimination by our very own government, you're more than welcome to do your own protest. However, we will miss you guys dearly, as this will be the only LGBTQ+ club on campus to not be in attendance."

The student sits back in her chair, obviously understanding the situation. "Right. We'll get started on our own member sign-up for the day then."

"Perfect. I'd like to thank you all for meeting with me today, and I look forward to working together in the future," I tell them, keeping my tone light.

As soon as the door shuts behind me, I let my smile drop. My phone vibrates in my pocket, matching the anxious vibrations under my skin. I don't know how Aaliyah does it, but I'll have to thank her for lending me her strength later.

There's a message from Isamu, a picture of Inu wearing my safety glasses—sans work vest—and another message from Gonzales, letting me know what time he's going to the court with another friend.

This will be the fourth time we've played together, and I've found myself looking forward to it. Only a little, because then finals will come, and we'll both be too busy to remember what friendship between us sounded like.

I react to the message of Inu with a thumbs up, and meet Gonzales and his friend Anthony at the basketball court after making a pit stop to change. My court shoes are ratty hand-me-downs from one of the kids down the road that I've had since I was a teenager. The toe has a hole in it, but I can't figure out if it's worse to leave it or duct tape them.

"Hey man," I clasp hands with Anthony, a scrawny, tall guy with a thick nest of brown hair, and take the ball that Gonzales passes. His pass is familiar by now, and I clutch the ball tightly to my chest, wondering if I could possibly be the type of person to have more than one friend. First Aaliyah, then Gonzales. I just don't know if Isamu sits in the category of friend, employer, or mere pit stop.

My shot misses the hoop; total air ball.

"Oof. And here I was just about to pick you for my IM team," Gonzales jokes.

I warm up my wrists by tossing the ball just above my head.

"You remember when we barely even needed a warm-up in high school? Oh, to be old," Anthony says, grunting as he gives a hard bounce pass to Gonzales.

Gonzales laughs at him and goes to make an easy layup, but is rejected by my own ball hitting the rim before bouncing out.

"Motherfucker," I mumble, annoyed that my shot got disrupted.

Anthony's right. It takes us a while to warm up but once we do, it's a free for all, each man on his own team. Anthony starts with the ball, but as I easily snatch it from his poor dribbling stance, Gonzales comes for me with a vengeance.

Despite the spring in my step, the speed of my crossover, and the heat of my desire to prove myself, Anthony and I are neck-and-neck.

"Travel," I call out, scoffing as Gonzales loses the ball again. "Stop playing like a post or he's gonna win," I complain.

"*Culero*, I'm already losing no matter what." Gonzales laughs, taking a step toward Anthony at the half court line. "At least I can't foul out," he says before batting at the ball and slapping Anthony tiredly.

"Watch it, man," Anthony says, unimpressed.

But the distraction was enough for me to come in and steal the ball. Since I'm already at the half court line, I can easily rush the basket for a breakaway layup.

"Dammit Gonzales," Anthony complains as I smirk at them.

"Hey, whatever works as long as you don't win." Gonzales pats my sweaty back. "Good shit, John."

I grunt and lift my shirt to wipe my face.

"Woah, that's one hell of a tattoo."

I pull my shirt back down at Anthony's words.

"What is it?" Gonzales asks. I glare at Gonzales, who shrugs.

"It's a portrait of Lou Rawls with a microphone," I say, leaving out that the other pec is an image of my mom dancing in our living room. It covers my entire chest, going just underneath my pecs.

"Who's that?" Anthony asks.

I think of the vinyl record sitting in my dad's record player at home. "He's a soul singer." I think of my mom dancing with him, me on my dad's shoulders.

"I've always wanted tattoos. Did it hurt?"

I look at Anthony and raise an eyebrow. "More than you can imagine," I tell him. "Anyway, if it's decided that I'm the best player here, I should head out."

"Woah, I wouldn't say the best," Gonzales complains.

I let a laugh escape, just barely so my teeth don't show. "I have to go help Isamu with the van." It's solar panel installation day and it's not a task anyone can do alone. Those panels are too big and awkward.

"Send him my love," Gonzales says. "And this." He smacks my ass.

I hesitate and look back at him. Anthony puts his head in his hands and groans.

"He's my lover, so give him a good spanking for me," Gonzales says with a wink.

I roll my eyes and throw a wave over my shoulder. "I'll make sure to tell Aaliyah she's old news."

Sweat drips down Isamu's soft abs as we rest against the van.

"I didn't realize they were that heavy," Isamu says, letting Inu lick the sweat from his palm. He runs a hand over her head and comes back with a palm full of black fur.

"Gross," I comment as Isamu wipes it off against his jeans.

He smirks and rubs it against my chest, leaving behind a tingling feeling.

"Here," I start, taking the shirt tucked into the side of his pants and wiping my hands on it. He makes a noise of complaint and I gesture at my fur-covered shirt. "We could probably get some of the cuts done today."

Isamu stares at the table saw. "How does it work?" He sounds exasperated and I think of the drill bits he was studying the first day.

"I left you safety glasses. Inu had them last?" I remind him.

Inu's head turns to me and I shy away from her.

"See? See that?" he gestures at me. "The way you feel about dogs is how I feel about putting my hands near a—a saw thing."

I huff out a laugh and shake my head. "Saw injuries happen because of human error. You just have to know how to use them."

"Johnny, Johnny, Johnny," he puts his hands against my shoulders. I should shy away from him as well, but I let Isamu linger as long as he wants. He'll let go eventually; everyone does. "Dog attacks happen because of human error too. That's what I'm saying."

He lets go.

"So, fear of the unknown?" I challenge, ignoring my own disappointment toward a feeling I should have grown used to.

He touches the tip of his nose to let me know I've understood.

"That why you're going on this trip? Facing your fears."

Isamu lets out a bark of laughter before turning and grabbing a slab of uncut wood. "Now we're getting somewhere too complicated, Johnny."

"I thought you were an open book," I tease, helping him put the wood on the table.

"Only about things I know about myself," he answers with an easy smile.

"Isn't your roommate a shrink? Whatever, let's just cut this wood." I turn to the table. "Okay, I get it looks intimidating, so just remember there are no dumb questions." It's verbatim what my shop teacher said in high school, but I just rather Isamu not use it and let me get it down quicker.

He sighs. "I feel like I'm going to put that to the test."

"Mm, maybe leave the cutting to me," I tell him.

Isamu scoots closer as I explain the safety guidelines and how the saw works. But the second I flip on the machine, he takes a shaky step backwards into Inu. I flip it off as he glances at his watch while Inu snuffles against his jeans.

Loud noises still get my dad sometimes too. Sometimes I wonder if that's part of the reason he felt like he had to be drunk at the shop.

"Here," I tell him, pulling out a pair of unopened ear plugs from my work pants. I keep them handy in case, but I never actually use them. It's too late to save me from tinnitus.

"Heh, I'm a mess," he says with a self-deprecating laugh.

"It's fine. My dad's the same."

"So, it doesn't get better?"

I shrug. "It's PTSD. It affects everyone differently, but it's definitely gotten . . . better. Easier? Manageable," I decide on.

Isamu doesn't look any more comfortable and I have to keep myself from reaching out a comforting hand. The ghost of his touch is still familiar, but I remind myself he's just a mere pit stop. Not someone I should be fighting to comfort.

"You're welcome to chill while I cut these?" I offer.

He shakes his head. "Nah, I got this."

We measure four times and cut once until we're out of wood and the sun is long set. I spend the entire time trying to ignore the way Isamu's proximity makes my heart clench and my throat close up.

Isamu

Inu lets out a bark just before Gonzales appears at my door, car keys in hand and a grin on his face. His hair is still wet from his shower.

"Come on. Let's go get some late-night munchies," he says, looking down at me.

I'm in the middle of an extensive excel sheet, reluctantly adding links to van parts. There are a lot of basic things that I thought I had covered but the further John and I get, the more I realize I'm missing pieces here and there.

This is the same sheet I've sent John three times now, and each time he finds something new to add, or mentions a part we may or may not need—but if we don't get it, we'll be sitting around for weeks waiting for shipping.

That's all the army was. Hurry up and wait. Being rushed to get something done and then finding you have nothing else to do.

At least this time, my company is easy on the eyes and entertaining to talk to.

"Where are we getting munchies?" I ask, slowly shutting my laptop so I can manhandle myself up from the floor and back into my prosthesis. Sometimes it's just easier to hop around the apartment than wear my leg all day.

Inu stands near me as I hop around.

"Ready?" Gonzales asks as soon as I'm up.

I look at him in disbelief. "I still need my leg, man."

"Why? Just grab your crutches and we can go like that, no?"

Being without my leg is vulnerable. Defenseless. It's walking into a gun fight with your hands tied behind your back. I'm still too shaky, too raw to go out without it—at least past the apartment front lawn. I still check every alleyway between buildings for muggers or worse. Loud noises still have me reaching for a gun that isn't there. Nightmares still have me in their death grip, and I wake up in a cold sweat from kicking my phantom foot as I try to get it out from falling rubble.

"Not comfy," I summarize for Gonzales, putting on my lining.

The night air is cooler than I expected, and I pull Inu a little closer, letting her fur warm me against North Carolina's ever-changing weather.

"Smells like winter," I say.

Gonzales gives me a funny look. "I thought I was the one who was supposed to be saying weird things after studying all night. Not you."

I laugh, casually draping my arm around him as I secretly steal his body heat too. Thank God for the Mustang.

"You ever been to Aaliyah's dorm?" I ask after settling Inu in the backseat.

He's never once mentioned going to her dorm. I would know; no matter how infatuated with her he is, the bitching would be endless if he saw how messy her dorm was—too much like his childhood.

I wonder what John's dorm looks like. Probably broody or lacking personality—it'd expose him too much. Even today, he looked like he was pulling teeth talking about his dad's PTSD. It's like taking apart one of those magnetic puzzles. Getting him to talk is like prying my fingernails between metal plates that I have to pull at so hard, I bleed a little.

Even still, I can't find the energy to stop as long as he's still willing.

"A few times," Gonzales responds. "Why?"

I hum, wondering what stance I'm supposed to take.

"Oh. I went the other day and it's . . . you know?"

I wonder if something like that would be a deal breaker for them. Some eccentricity about one of them that drives the other insane. But isn't love supposed to be loving someone despite those eccentricities? Because of? Not that I would know. I've never had time for anything but soul crushing hookups that leave me staring at my phone afterwards, wondering if I'll get a text.

"*Oralé*," Gonzales starts with a laugh. "She's a little messy, huh?"

"It doesn't bother you?" I ask.

Gonzales grins from the driver seat. "Sure does but . . . people are complicated and her mess is... well." He parks at the gas station. "It's like this," he starts, speaking with his hands. "I'm clean and organized because my childhood never was."

I nod, remembering the credit card purchases strewn all over the floor, along with a long line of his mom's heavy-handed lovers, who I didn't know about until Gonzales showed up at my house one night.

"I longed for something different. Better. My cleanliness reflects the me within: calm, patient, organized. Aaliyah is messy—"

"—because her parents were strict," I supply.

"Sure," he says, making a so-so gesture. "And controlling and expecting her—the woman—to clean and be organized. So, yeah, it looks messy, but it's actually her just taking control of her life."

I smirk, impressed and in awe of my best friend's blanket acceptance. "And, let me ask, does she know you've shrinked her?"

He frowns and looks down at his hands guiltily. "No, uh, definitely not. Most people aren't fans of it."

"Huh, you don't say," I tease, hiding the discomfort I feel. "Do you shrink me?"

Gonzales gets out of the car quickly. A shiver runs up my spine at the feeling of being watched by him. I wonder what my room says about me and if I even want to know. Probably not and by now, I've gotten used to everyone's eyes on me, making sure I'm okay.

I hop out quickly and get Inu. She gives me a searching gaze when she jumps out, and I smile down at her—anything to get my serious child excited. Running my hand over her fur, I lead her into the store, dirty glass doors sliding open as we approach.

"No dogs," the attendant says, her voice coarser than Inu's fur from years of smoking.

Good thing I'm on a quitting cycle.

"She's a service animal," I tell her.

She rolls her eyes and slaps her magazine on the counter. Her tired eyes roam over me as my skin prickles. Pulling Inu tight against my leg, I stare her down.

"Whatever, kid," she says. "You can do whatever you want."

Gonzales grabs my bicep and I turn my steely glare away from her. His grip is tight as he manhandles me to the drinks.

"What, man?" I ask, ripping my arm from him.

"If you didn't tell her off, I would've. Then she would've called the cops, and I'm too brown for that, güey," he says, aggressively grabbing an energy drink from behind the glass.

There have been stares on the bus and in the grocery stores, and little children running up to Inu to pet her. A few times, people have even asked me why I need a service dog, but each time it grates on my nerves a little.

These people don't deserve to know my pain. They don't need to probe at my weak points just to feel better about themselves. Just leave me alone and let me not feel so inadequate.

Maybe John isn't such a puzzle after all.

Chapter Seven

John

THE BEST THING ABOUT my day has become working at the storage unit with Isamu. It's the most relaxing break that I could ask for in my busy schedule. Isamu is bent over the table saw, cutting what will soon become the cabinets of his van, while I lick sauce off my bento box.

Of all the jobs I've worked, I've never worked one where my employer does more work than I do. But Isamu has stuck to his word; he only asks for help when he needs it, but otherwise leaves me to my devices—unless he wants to talk my ear off.

I flick on my Polaroid camera and capture the empty dog bed in the corner. I'm trying not to find some deep meaning in it—trying not to be one of those types of artsy folks—but there's something sickeningly satisfying about watching Inu never use it. I can put a pin in that and let my therapist dissect tomorrow.

"You get any good shots of her?" Isamu asks, the table saw quiet.

I look over at him, snapping the little rectangle film between two fingers as it develops.

"Nah, sorry. I don't really take pictures of people… or dogs."

He gives me a contemplative look that I meet with an unenthused one. I have therapy tomorrow; the last thing I want is to have a secret sharing session right now. Being scrubbed raw in therapy once a month is enough for me, and since Isamu came into my life, it feels like my emotions have been scattered.

"I want to ask why, but you're glaring at me like if I do, you might put my head on this table saw next," he says with a teasing grin before turning away to grab a new piece of wood. "What can I ask you that you'll answer right now?"

The table saw starts up again, purposefully giving me time to think about it. I think, if a gun was pressed to my head, I could write an entire autobiography of photos. But not a single one would contain a picture of a person.

The thing is, life is not permanent. It ends in a guaranteed final breath. A moment where everything about us ceases to exist. I don't care about that moment, or anything after. I care about this, right now. That probably wouldn't make sense if someone saw my photos. They're grainy, broken, poorly lit. But maybe I don't want a clear shot. Maybe I don't want to remember my dad showing up to my middle school graduation drunk, and after I yelled at him until I was lightheaded, not showing up at all to my high school one.

But I want to remember him.

It doesn't make sense to me. I've wished he would die—a dark wish only made at the lowest points—and I've watched him nearly succeed in fulfilling that cold, dark wish just as many times.

All that hatred, yet I still love him.

So, the photos. They're like a hazy memory of my life. The only way my life can be made palatable.

But when the table saw finally shuts off, all I can say is, "I always take the best photos with my other camera."

"What are the best photos?" Isamu asks, looking away as he aligns the newly cut wood.

"In the Appalachians, when it's cold like this, the leaves start falling and everything becomes this explosion of autumn. It's my favorite time of year, but I doubt I'll be able to make it this year with school and work."

Isamu turns back toward me and purses his lips. I watch, with something akin to horror, as his face breaks out into a sly grin.

I don't allow myself too many comforts in life—I'm generally too busy for it. But, once a month, I pack a blanket into my backpack and sit on the soft velvety couch across from my therapist to bitch about life.

"So, you're frustrated because your friend asked you to call out of work to visit the mountains with the rest of your friends?" Dr. Little asks, eyebrows raised.

I fight the urge to pull the couch pillow against my chest and groan.

"My client, and I'm frustrated because I don't have the budget flexibility to take time off work," I tell him honestly.

"John, I know we've talked about this before, but there's no shame in taking more than four years to finish your degree. You could take less classes and rest more, or take a co-op and work to save money during the school year."

I wave the notion away. I just want to get this over with as quickly as possible. Only two years left.

Dr. Little smiles at my brush off. He's used to me by now.

"Okay, well then, let's just focus on your frustration. Do you not want to go with your friend—"

"Isamu."

"Isamu," Dr. Little says. "Do you not want to go with him?"

I bobble my head back and forth. "I want to see the leaves. Honestly, he kind of... he's always trying to get to know me," I explain, frustrated.

"And that bothers you." He doesn't even ask. He knows it does. He's sat on the chair for two years now and never gotten me to talk about my mom other than the fact that she's gone. It took him a whole year to learn about my dad. Something Isamu achieved in almost a night.

"Yes. But what bothers me the most is I actually keep telling him stuff." It's like he knows exactly what parts of the dam to poke at to get a trickle of water. He's just not ready for the onslaught if he ever makes the dam break.

Dr. Little hums and gives me another arching eyebrow, waiting for me to understand some meaning hidden behind my words that I don't see yet. CBT—Cognitive Behavioral Therapy—is all about giving me the tools to handle my own brain, but it just feels like I'm teetering between an exam and a lobotomy sometimes.

When he sees that I'm not getting it, he sighs—not unkindly—and scoots forward.

"Do you think maybe the reason you're telling him stuff is because you want to let him in?"

I scoff and shake my head. A pit stop in life is not the same as letting someone into your life.

"I'll give it thought." I watch the clock on the wall flip, telling me our time is up.

Isamu

John's camera bag is sitting on top of the picnic basket I packed. I can't tear my eyes away from it; it feels like every secret about him is poured into whatever he secretly takes photos of. It's like that camera is attached to his soul.

How much can you know about a person based solely on the secrets they keep?

I don't hear John approach behind me until it's too late, and I take a quick step backward to hide my prying. When I played basketball, I'd watch teammates and opponents stumble and fall, and always wonder why they didn't catch themselves. But now, it happens so fast that I don't realize I'm falling. Before I know it, I've tripped on John's foot and suddenly I'm on top of him.

Thighs. Chest. Arms. Groin. All of mine pressed against him as I bear all my weight on him. Like heat but everywhere and deeper than just skin. His breath sweeps against my hair. His calloused hand slides against my bare waist, where my shirt slid up, to steady me. His heart beats rapidly in his chest pressed so tightly against mine.

A roaring that isn't just my ears makes both of our necks snap to the storage unit opening, where Gonzales's Mustang is pulling up. John makes a noise of discomfort and I quickly roll off him, face aflame at my own stupidity.

Inu comes over and snuffles against my chest as I sit on the floor, while John scrambles up.

Gonzales smirks at me when he gets out of the Mustang, Aaliyah on his heels. I glare back, begging him not to point out my blush.

"Ready to get a move on?" Gonzales asks, clasping John's hand and bringing him into a hug.

"You sure your Mustang can handle the curves?" I ask, attempting to distract myself from the flex of John's arms, thighs, hips.

Gonzales turns and blinks at me slowly, while a sly grin splits John's face.

"His what?" John asks slowly.

"His... car? I mean, I know it's not like any of us have a better option. I just wasn't sure that it could handle the curves in the mountains. Those roads get tiny, you know?"

"Yeah, but what type of car is it?" Aaliyah asks, hand pressed to her mouth.

"A Mustang," I say tentatively, suddenly unsure.

John turns to grab his camera bag, laughing. I keep my eyes trained on Gonzales, so I don't have to pretend I'm not checking him out. Inu nuzzles me again, but there isn't a way for me to tell her my heart rate is elevated for reasons that aren't PTSD responses right now.

"Isa. *Pollito. Amor.* You think this is a Mustang?" Gonzales asks, pointing at his car.

I shrug and pop open the trunk to put the picnic basket in. "Is that not—" But it's obvious it's not a Mustang. "What is it?" I ask instead.

Aaliyah laughs and gets into the backseat. I open the other backseat door, commanding Inu inside before following her. My knees are pressed to the back of John's seat and I regret ever suggesting we spend two hours cooped up in a car together. I can't stop thinking about his body against mine. Sturdy. Rugged. There are too many ways to describe it that I can't even put into thought without erupting into a blush again.

"What type of car is it?" I ask again as Gonzales gets in and starts it up, the engine roaring.

His radio is playing some soft pop.

"This is a 1969 Camaro. It's a classic, Isa."

I huff and sit back in my seat, still not understanding the difference or why it matters.

Aaliyah begins to whine as John starts to explain why a Camaro is different than a Mustang. I understand her half-hearted complaints when, an hour later, he and Gonzales are gushing over the "beautiful intricacies" that differentiate a 1969 Camaro from any of the following versions.

I can barely see John, but the excitement in his voice is palpable. If I had known cars were the way to get him to talk, I would've taken researching vans more seriously.

Gonzales groans as his phone rings, knowing his and John's car talk is coming to a close.

John picks up the phone from where it's connected to the aux cord on the upgraded stereo.

"It's a random phone number," John says, voice monotone now that it's something he doesn't have the energy for. "Probably a spam caller."

I lean forward, putting my arm on Inu. She glares at me from the corner of her eyes, but I look away and reach for the phone before answering the call.

"Hi, thank you for calling Bojangles. How may I help you?" I ask in my most upbeat customer service voice I can muster.

"Isamu," starts a warm, accented falsetto voice. "Can you give the phone to *Chuchito*?"

My insides turn to cold liquid as Gonzales's childhood nickname rings through the speaker. He lightly presses the brakes, his hands gripping the steering wheel as if he could choke the life out of it.

"He's not here right now," I say, leaning further to put my hand on Gonzales's shoulder as he pulls off the road and puts his head against the steering wheel.

Gonzales's mom sighs on the other end of the phone, and I wonder if I should pull the aux cord out of the phone to save everyone from hearing whatever comes next.

"Tell him to stop being—" she pauses in anger, searching for the words in Spanish. I was there for enough fights in our childhood to know most of them were in a language I didn't understand.

"We're expecting him at Thanksgiving dinner," she ends up saying.

Gonzales slowly reaches for his phone, still clutched in my hand, and presses end on the call.

"I thought you had her number blocked," I say because the silence is stifling. John is silent, gazing out the window as if he wants to be anywhere but here, but Aaliyah is clenched tight, protectiveness over her boyfriend making her a fierce figure.

"I do. It's a new one." Gonzales groans and leans his head back on the seat before reaching back for Aaliyah's hand. It looks uncomfortable as he twists their fingers together, but I still wish I had that domesticity with someone.

When Gonzales came to my door with his sister, I can't say I was surprised. I knew he and his mom had a tough relationship. I just never knew the entire extent of what was happening.

"Do you want to talk about it?" Aaliyah asks.

"I can step out, if you want?" John offers, already undoing his seatbelt, always eager to leave when things get emotionally vulnerable.

"No, John. It's fine," Gonzales says. "Yeah, Liyah. Just give me a second. I'm really mad right now, and I don't want to be."

My anxious mouth fights the urge to make fun of Gonzales for having such a handle on his emotions. It might add to my own anxiety that he makes me feel so out of touch with my emotions.

Inu gets up and I have to shift off her. She sniffs me, then sits back down when she realizes the elevated heart rate she's smelling isn't coming from me. I know she isn't supposed to comfort anyone else, but a car isn't really the best place for me provide physical comfort to my best friend, and it makes me kind of wish Inu would instead.

"So. My mom," Gonzales starts with a deep breath. "Liyah, I know I've told you we're not in contact, but—" he sighs. "There's a reason for it."

From the back seat, I watch John tug on his sweater zipper before looking out the window, resigned.

"We left Mexico because it was dangerous, yada, yada, but when we got here, we were alone. I mean y'all know how Mexicans are treated in the US." He scoffs. "Land of immigrants, yeah right. I was too young to remember, but we really struggled getting on our feet here. It was just the three of us: my mom, me, and my little sister. Until my mom started dating. Some of them were fine; most of them weren't, but I thought she was just putting up with it to get us stuff. I turned a blind eye to it, you know the struggle of a single mom. And we got lots of stuff, toys, new kitchen appliances, you name it." He runs a hand down his face.

I place my hand on his shoulder. It's a little awkward when he's holding Aaliyah's hand and I have to reach over Inu, but he gives me an appreciative smile.

"I didn't find out until I started applying for scholarships my sophomore year—getting ahead of the curve—that my mom had been taking out credit cards in my name. A lot of credit cards." He pulls his hand away from Aaliyah and squeezes his hands in frustration. "She took out shady loans from shady people with my name. Fucked me before I was even out of the gate. I wouldn't even be in college if it weren't for Isamu's trust fund." He turns around and smirks at me. "*Pinche* rich people."

I give him a soft smile back. I remember us—my dad, mom, me, and Gonzales—sitting around the kitchen table, offering to send him to college with the money my parents had put away. It's not like I had ever planned on attending and if I changed my mind, the government would pay for it.

Gonzales is family. My parents knew that from childhood when he'd show up early to our playdates and stay days on end. He's never left my side and provided me a childhood I never could've had as an only child.

"I sued her for every penny she spent and more. Paid off all the credit cards, bought this Camaro with the leftovers, and ruined my mom's life. My sister doesn't talk to me anymore because she sees it as a necessary risk, considering it was those loans that helped us afford a house in the rich kid neighborhood.

"So, yeah. That's my family."

Aaliyah leans over and hugs him from behind. "Thank you for telling us that. I know sorry doesn't mean anything, but I am nonetheless. You know my dad's a politician who signs anti-trans bills and hates LGBTQ+ people, so if you ever want to bitch about families, I'm here for you."

I smile, happy to see my brother connect with someone so deeply. Someone who understands him and won't ever make him feel like he's in the wrong. It makes my decision to venture off easier. I know he's in good hands.

Aaliyah reaches out and pats John's hand. "John's really good at listening, so you can talk to him too."

"Yep," he adds, ever the chatterbox.

I snort and then quickly try to cover it up with my words. "Gonzales, you know my family will always be here for you—your family really. You're my brother, man. I really do want to be there for you. Thick and thin."

I turn to John when I feel his gaze on me, and am surprised by his furrowed eyebrows. He's asking me a question, but I'm disappointed to find out I don't know him well enough to know what. I want to know him fully.

"Appreciate that, Isa. I just... I'm glad I have your parents at least."

"My parents are awesome. Unlike yours," I say with a grin.

Gonzales turns around and punches my knee with a smile—unfortunately, the wrong one.

"Shit!" He clutches his hand as I cackle in the backseat. "I think I broke my hand," he complains, looking down at the knuckles.

"Call me Bionic Man; I have superpowers that include not being punchable."

Gonzales turns around, fist raised teasingly. "Bring your face closer and we'll see about that."

I continue to laugh as Gonzales turns back around. The Piedmont gets left behind, making way for the soft mountains erupting in colorful trees as we wind down the beautiful roads of North Carolina.

Chapter Eight

John

MIDTERMS ARE IN full swing and I've taken the week off from any form of work. Apparently, that doesn't mean work has taken the week off from me.

"Where's Inu?" I ask Isamu, where he's made himself

comfortable by draping himself over my bed, tossing a tennis ball over his head. He's so at ease despite never having been here before. He looks like he belongs there, pretty and obnoxious like he's been every day since I've met him. Too bad these days are limited.

"Gave her the day off. She's a hard worker; too serious. I worry she doesn't get enough time to be a kid." He flicks the ball against the wall near my head and smirks at my annoyance. "Am I disturbing your studying?"

I turn back toward my desk. The truth is, there isn't any more studying to do. I've spent weeks exhausting myself to keep up and accidentally put myself ahead of the curve. There's only so many more practice exams I can do.

"Yeah, deeply. Where's your boyfriend?"

"Gonzales," Isamu says pointedly, "is with Aaliyah studying for something or another."

"Is studying a strong choice of words?"

Isamu snorts and continues to toss the ball. "Oh yeah. They're definitely taking more study breaks than studying. What about you, Johnny boy? Where's your girlfriend?"

This would be the perfect opportunity to tell Isamu. I'm gay—slip it out there nice and easy. It wouldn't even sound forced or like I'm interested in my client. Which I'm not.

"I'm not aromantic, but I don't date," I tell him truthfully. I don't fuck around with people that are just going to leave me. Which is to say, I don't fuck around with people at all.

"Ha! Of course you don't. Ever so mysterious. Do you get a gold star every time you say something angsty?"

"Do you get a gold star every time you're a dick?" I shoot back, annoyed.

He sits up quickly, smile quickly dropping off his face. "Sorry, got ahead of myself. I envy this," he waves his hand over my general vicinity. "Whole introspective thing you have going on. I actually get it, you know. It's easier to not get hurt if you don't open up," he finishes, laying back on my bed.

"You okay?" I ask, willing to let go of his barb now that I know where it comes from.

He hums in thought and flicks the ball back up.

"I've been thinking—"

"Dangerous," I cut in.

"I've been thinking," he trucks on, ignoring me. "About that thing you said. 'Fear of the unknown.' It was one of the many times we were cutting wood."

"Yeah, I remember." I slide my papers into my desk drawer, knowing they're not getting touched for the rest of today.

"I feel like I should be having this conversation with Gonzales—fucking psych majors—but... I don't know. You get me. Or, no, you just don't care?"

"I don't judge?" I supply.

Isamu nods readily. "And you're not going to give me advice. You're just going to... listen. Or not. You're like Inu 2.0."

"How so?" I straddle my desk chair, ready for whatever Isamu is going to give me.

He laughs and rubs the back of his neck, looking away with a blush. "Uh, I talk to her all day. Like all day. She doesn't respond but it's nice."

"Maybe that's why she's so serious. She realizes you're a mess and she has to be the adult." I grin at him.

He launches the ball at the wall near me again. "You're so obnoxious," he says through a laugh. "Shh, seriously. I'm going to be introspective." He waves his hands grandly above his head, still laying on the bed. "Let me channel my inner John."

"Go for it," I challenge.

He sighs. "What if I'm traveling because I'm scared?"

I don't respond.

"Like, uh—man, I gotta be stoned for this. What if my dad still looks at me like I came back broken, and my roommate-slash-best friend is secretly psychoanalyzing me, and what if I just want to travel because everything here is falling apart, but in reality, it's me that's fallen apart?"

He throws the ball.

"That still doesn't feel right."

"It feels closer," I tell him, and he shrugs.

"It does. How do I say it in an angsty John way?" He looks up at me and grins, his chin bunching up unattractively against his neck. It almost makes me smile.

"You don't say anything," I tell him, honestly.

"Does that get lonely?"

I think about it: if I feel alone; lonesome.

"Sometimes." When my dad was too drunk and I was too small to carry him. When Isamu sits in my bed and talks about feelings, but I feel like there's Carolina tar in my throat keeping me from doing the same. "But most of the time, it doesn't."

"Do you get tired of holding everything in your head without anyone to help?"

I'm not sure I'd trust anyone to. If it's too much for me to deal with, how could anyone else? I think of Isamu holding Gonzales up while he was running from his mom. I wonder if Isamu could bear the weight of all of my troubles, but I know that he can't. No one can. That's why they all leave.

"I don't know what you mean, Isa," I tell him, leaning my cheek against the chair.

He smiles. "Now you're calling me that, too?"

"Should I not?"

"No, please do. It's like my baby nickname though, so it's funny to hear it from you." He flicks up the ball but misses the catch.

It hits him in the face but we both ignore it. "Do you ever . . . want people in your life?" he asks. "To help shoulder the burden? To take on dates? Share a bed with or a meal?"

I glance at the bento box Isamu brought me earlier, sitting on my bedside table, and push away the desire.

"Seems kind of cruel to expect that," I tell him.

"I'm sure someone would want to. I hope someone would help shoulder my . . . Isamuness."

Words are hard. Saying things that are going to be thrown away the second Isamu leaves is harder.

Grunting, I stand from my desk chair. "Well, you aren't going to find romance sitting in my room moping. Food?"

Isamu turns down Twinnie's, and Cosmic, and every other suggestion I make until we wind up at his apartment, loudly making ourselves known in fear of walking in on Aaliyah and Gonzales. It's all for naught, however. Aaliyah and Gonzales stare up at us from the kitchen table with matching looks of annoyance.

"Couldn't be sure," Isamu says with a shrug before going into the kitchen.

I look over Aaliyah's shoulder and peer at her studies. "Ah yes, vector calculus. One of the many calculi that every common man should know."

She grabs my chin, her long nails scratching nicely at my itchy beard. "John, I have literally been doing this for five hours straight. Please tell me you come with food."

"I'm making it as we speak," Isamu calls from the kitchen.

Gonzales groans, stands with a luxurious stretch, and follows Isamu's voice to the kitchen. "I should give him a hand."

"Where did we find two hot men that could cook?" Aaliyah asks quietly, pushing her cheek against mine, still holding my chin.

I hum and push away from her. "Don't get it twisted," I tell her, sitting at the table.

Inu trots in from the hallway and pauses to sniff at Aaliyah. Aaliyah gives Inu a practiced scratched between her ears.

"What do you mean? You guys are together all the time and you're gonna tell me you're not even a little interested."

I shrug at Aaliyah, knowing if I tell her that my eyes can't seem to stop seeking out Isamu and my hands itch to reach out, then she won't let it go. Isamu is just a stranger making a pit stop; I have to convince myself to let him go as quickly as he'll let *me* go.

Inu comes over and stares at me. I stare back. She lays by my feet, and I cede the little space I have so she can rest her head gently over her paws.

"It's not like that," I tell Aaliyah.

She gives a pointed look at Inu, then toward the kitchen. "He's making you food."

Rolling my eyes, I push Aaliyah's papers toward her, hoping she'll let it distract her. It's best not to tell her he makes me food almost every day.

She pushes it away. "I'm not saying every gay guy is an option, John. I'm just saying, he is making you dinner." Her eyes widen and her grin grows mischievous, but I'm already shaking my head.

"It's just friendly. He doesn't know I'm gay."

I'm already putting my hands over Aaliyah's mouth when she gasps, used to her dramatics. I blame her roommate Keelie; she's been slowly making Aaliyah more and more boy-crazy over the years.

"Bitch, how?" she asks.

I laugh and shake my head. "Bitch, because I don't do relationships."

She leans back and frowns. "Do you want to? Like with him."

"No," I say, my voice sounding certain despite my gut twisting.

I frown down at the table, ignoring my discomfort. "Does Gonzales ever make you dinner or do you just leave the whip cream for post-study activities?" I ask with a smirk.

She takes the bait but for some reason, I find that for the first time, I wish she hadn't.

Isamu

Gonzales stands over me, looming and annoying, as I cut onions. The onions are making his eyes water—mine are long used to it. He sniffles, I cut.

"What?" I finally ask. "Are you helping me or just being creepy?"

He laughs, sniffles, and grabs a pair of pork cutlets.

"Mexican or Japanese?" he asks, salting each piece of meat.

"Uh, I don't know. We could do spicy cutlets?"

He leans against the counter and we stare at each other.

"Slice the pork? Make tofu, add some peppers with the seeds and ginger?" I ask, staring at the fridge as I try to think of everything we might have in there.

"Ginger to calm the stomach from all the spicy?" Gonzales grins.

"Does... Aaliyah? Actually," I can't remember if John likes spice, so I stick my head out of the kitchen to ask. "Is spicy—" both of their heads snap up, looking oddly guilty.

"Spice? Yes, no?" I hold my hand up, flipping between thumb up and thumb down.

"Like Cholula?" Aaliyah asks.

Gonzales snorts from the kitchen.

"Sure. Is Cholula too much spice or too little?"

Aaliyah looks at John. He shrugs. They whisper something to each other and I continue to stand there—thumb up, thumb down, decision unmade.

"Too little. I can go hotter," Aaliyah says.

John immediately puts his head in his hands and I grow concerned. "John, that okay?"

"If it's not hotter than Gumbo, I think I'm set," he mumbles, pulling his head up only to motion at Aaliyah and shake his head.

I'm proud to realize I understand John's mannerisms well enough to know he's saying she can't handle the spice.

"We've got Cayenne peppers," I murmur to myself returning to the fridge. I hand Gonzales a few and he snorts.

"This is more than Cholula," he says but starts cutting anyway.

"Just don't put any in hers. We have bell peppers too."

The smells of spice fill the kitchen and Gonzales and I continuously adjust the Japanese tacos as we take samples from each other's sides. If my dad were here, he'd be drinking ginger tea—more milk than tea—just to make it through.

"Was that... too much Cayenne you think?" I ask as I wipe the sweat from my brow after a bite.

Gonzales coughs into a napkin. "Nah," he starts, voice raspy. "It's good shit but I'm definitely calling dibs on the toilet afterwards."

"Solid," I tell him, plating the dishes, making sure I know which hand has Aaliyah's tacos in it.

Inu is, surprisingly, under John when we get to the table. But even more surprisingly, John seems cool and collected, despite her just being inches away. It's not hard to notice that he's grown more used to her while we work on the van conversion. But while I've been letting my hands linger against John's while passing him fifty different types of screwdrivers, maybe they've grown closer than I thought.

Seeing them so close to each other twists my gut in a way that feels like falling and being held all at once. I almost think about switching my plate with Aaliyah's less spicy one until I remind myself John is straight. Now my guts are just falling, quite pathetically falling.

"This isn't even spicy," Aaliyah says triumphantly as she finishes her first taco.

John has been steadily eating his, eyes glued to mine, squinted and goading. I smirk at him as I take another bite, ignoring the bead of sweat that drips down the side of my face. He shakes his head and takes another bite.

Gonzales is long past tapped out, swirling milk in his mouth between bites but carrying on delightedly anyway.

"Are you guys sweating? This is nothing," Aaliyah says proudly. "Man, and I always thought I was such a wuss for spice."

John bites his lip, raising an eyebrow at me. I shrug and take another bite that sears my tongue, but not so much that I can't taste the flavor underneath the burn. It's sweetened and offset by the tofu infused with ginger sugar broth.

"Aaliyah, *tesoro*, can you get me more milk?" Gonzales begs.

She pops another bite into her mouth and nods. John finally looks away from me when Aaliyah comes back with a Cayenne pepper in hand.

"Can you eat these whole?"

Immediately, we're all making noises of disagreement.

"But they're kind of sweet," she argues, handing Gonzales his milk. He chugs it down straight from the bottle. I stare in disgust.

"Liyah—" John starts, before stopping and just shaking his head.

Aaliyah looks on suspiciously, crossing her arms slowly.

"Why are you guys sweating?"

John stuffs his mouth and looks down at his plate, tapping out of the conversation. She isn't my girlfriend, so I turn away from the conversation, expecting Gonzales to nut up. He just continues on with his milk.

"Are you guys serious?" She lunges for one of Gonzales's tacos needlessly—he doesn't even fight her on it—and takes a bite.

John and I continue our stare off as soon as Aaliyah spits the bite into a napkin.

"Why did you make mine softer?" she asks, annoyed.

Gonzales finally takes a breath. "You thought Cholula was spicy, but if it makes you feel better, I'd rather have yours."

John and I get through our second taco. There's only one left. He takes the first bite, my stomach rolls; sweat drips into my eyes; John's barely even bothered.

"Is this like a pissing match?" Aaliyah asks, steering clear of Gonzales and his groaning.

"That's exactly what it is," he tells her.

John takes another bite. I hesitate, trying not to eyeball the milk. My eyes are watering but if I wipe them, I'll risk getting seeds in my eyes. I take a bite.

John grins and slowly, ever so cruel, puts the entire soft taco into his mouth. I blanch and breathe deeply in through my nose before doing the same.

He chews slowly and calmly. I spit it out into the napkin and reach for the jug of milk.

"Well, this has been fantastic," John says standing up. "Thank you both for the meal, but I should probably get back to studying."

He pats my sweaty back on the way out as I drink from the milk jug.

"*Pinche*, John. Where'd you find him, Aaliyah?" Gonzales asks.

I groan and lay my head on the table just as Inu comes and snuffles against my leg, even off duty, she can smell and hear my heart beating out of control. I just wish I could blame it on the tacos.

Chapter Nine

John

"WHAT?" I ASK INTO THE phone again, barely able to hear Isamu over the teasing of my coworkers.

"Today," he repeats, sounding as frustrated as I feel. He's better at showing his emotions that way.

"Instead of working on the van?" I ask, confused as to why he'd not want to work on the van he's paying me to build.

He laughs. "You've just finished your midterms and you're dying to get back to work."

I don't respond. I'm still reeling, not finding the angle here.

"Come on, Johnny," he says softly. "You, me, Inu—who I can tell you're starting to warm up to—"

If he means I've begun to trust her enough to not bite me while my back is turned, then he may be onto something.

"—and a bento. I made sushi."

"The Duke Gardens?" I ask, checking my watch.

"Yeah," Isamu clarifies. "Pick me up when you're done with work." Then he hangs up.

So, I pick him up when I'm done with work. The sun is starting to set earlier and earlier, and soon there won't be a sun for me except during my walk to class. For now, it shines on Isamu's hair, matching his dog's own onyx black fur as they get into my car.

"You acted so suspicious on the phone, man. It's like you'd think I'd take you to the gardens just to murder you."

I scoff. "As if you could."

Isamu looks at me, sizing me up and then leans over the center console excitedly. "Do you think you could take me in a fight?"

I hesitate. I'm a lot stockier and have maybe forty or more pounds on him, but he has military combat training.

"Ha! Absolutely, with your scrawny ass?" I lie. "You wouldn't stand a chance." He's not scrawny and I hate that I've noticed that.

"Yeah? What'd you like, play football in high school? Or nah, it had to be something that kept you from playing basketball, so wrestling?"

I smile, lips pressed hard against my crooked teeth. High school and anything before is what I consider the hardest time in my life. Baggy sweatshirts and keeping my head low, just hoping someday I'd get out of there. Out of here.

I'd go days without speaking to a single person, unwilling to make nice with teachers I argued with, starting from the first day of school and shunned by the students in my class, except for the few other outcasts I had nothing in common with. Then I'd go home, only to end my day at an empty house or a father falling over drunk.

Depression is the word that spikes up when I think of that time, but it was more like longing. Longing for it to end—but not my life, just that time of my life. Eighteen looked so far away. College seemed impossible. The John that I am now was just a pipe dream.

"Sorry, was that too hard of a question for your pea-sized brain?"

Isamu asks, snapping me out of my thoughts.

I shoot him a glare, just as we park outside of the Duke Gardens. "Okay, listen. You can take me in a fight, but I have a perfectly average-sized brain with lots of wrinkles on it, so hush."

"Hush," he repeats mockingly, but I'm already out of the car.

He opens the door for Inu—where she lays on old stains on the back seat—and calls for her to get out.

The air is tacky against my skin where my camera bag presses against my chest. I adjust it to drape over my hip as I watch Isamu stretch out his thigh, where his prosthesis attaches. His knuckles dig into a place high on his leg, and I wonder if he's okay to walk around the gardens. But Isamu is grown enough to know when he can and can't do something. And from the time I've spent around my dad's buddies, almost exclusively combat vets, I know there's no actual benefit to making someone feel less than.

"There's this place in the middle where I like to sit out and read sometimes," *when the weather is nicer*. "We can go there. At your pace," I tack on, because my bleeding heart can't stop its concern for Isamu despite my brain's attempts to shut it off.

"Hmm. Alright, let's go." He hands Inu her leash to give himself more room to carry the bag of food.

She trots along beside us, proudly carrying it in her jaw. She's not as tough and violent as she seemed to me at first.

"Hold up, there's some glass here."

I'm surprised to discover that Isamu is right. Duke is normally a spotless campus, tended to by proud students and a private university budget. But I suppose things slip every once in a while, especially since a lot of tourists come to the gardens.

Isamu plops down on his butt in the middle of the sidewalk, Inu beside him as he rifles through one of the satchels on the side of her bag.

"Found them," he says, triumphantly holding a pair of dog shoes.

"Oh, they're so small. They're like baby boots," I coo, awed at their small size.

Isamu looks up at me, a surprised grin on his face, eyebrows so high on his forehead that they're invisible under his recently growing bangs. I give him a blank stare in response. Partly, because I can coo at baby boots if I so please, the other part, because I don't know how to react to cooing at doggy boots—it's not something I make a habit of.

"Cute," Isamu mumbles under his breath when he turns back to Inu.

I'd like to say, because I'm such a solitary man-whore, who has received my fair share of compliments from the grimiest gay dating app in existence, it doesn't affect me. I'd like to say that. But I can't, because Isamu definitely doesn't realize he's said it loud enough for me to hear. Which means it isn't for flattery. It isn't a throwaway compliment to get in my pants. He doesn't even know I'm gay.

It's masochistic that I've kept it to myself for so long, but the second I tell him, everything changes. I open the door to potential that I've hidden from for so long. But the thought does bounce around in my brain. Repeatedly. Exhaustingly. Until the sound of Inu stamping her foot makes me look up and I realize all at once that I'm a raging idiot.

Of course, Isamu was calling Inu cute.

Behind them, I press my closed fist into my face, hiding my self-deprecating smile. All at once, I feel like a child again, being handed hope in the form of a teacher that seems to care—until later when she snaps at me to stop zoning-out during class. In the form of a classmate who tells me they like my handwriting until they tack on "it's very feminine" at the end. How foolish of me to see something nice and not think the box would snap from my fingers the second I try to grab it.

Luckily, I'm not a child anymore. It's easier to brush off now. Easier to put behind a wall built on years of not caring.

It's easier to slip on the mask with strangers. Isamu still counts as a stranger or, at least, that's what I tell myself as I follow him into the gardens.

He looks up at the sign below the garden entrance. It says no dogs allowed.

"That's just for pets," I tell him, unsure why he's hesitant. "Inu won't have any problems."

His jaw clenches as his whole body flexes, preparing to fight a battle that I can't even see. I look behind us, at the students touring campus with their parents and the professors, still on campus because of their research, taking a quick break.

"She'll be fine, Isamu," I say, softening my voice to comfort whatever battle it is.

He looks over at me and sighs. Despite his shorter legs, I have to hustle to catch up to him.

The gardens are less exciting now that fall has set in. I miss the smell of flowers that always permeates as the vast pink and yellow flowers blossom. But the park is still nice, flower beds matching the gothic style of the campus, trees aching to bend in the wind, and cultural displays from around the world scattered across the field.

I never dreamt I'd actually make it to Duke. Sometimes I feel like I'm here by accident. All the clubs listed on my application were true, but I was always the silent one, tucked in the back corner of the student's government classroom or art club. My grades in my IB classes were high, but other students had higher. Duke wasn't in the cards for me.

Isamu, on the other hand, has probably seen the gardens a million times, as he joined his own father on campus strolls. He had the privilege of growing up in a place people dream of going their whole lives.

"Did you ever think of going to Duke?" I ask as the breeze picks up against my threadbare jacket.

He laughs. "Fuck no. I wasn't even close to having the grades for it. I, er, well I was kind of the class clown."

I can picture it. Even now, Isamu is sociable, easy to look over my spikey exterior and still look for a friend. He cares so easily, and tries so hard to put a smile on my face that I try so hard to keep off.

Isamu looks over at me, his black eyes reflecting everything back onto me, a bold mirror into myself, and says, "Secret for a secret?"

There's so much more I'm holding onto, even as I slowly unravel a million tiny things I've kept hidden from everyone, just for Isamu. I'm afraid the more I give him, the harder it will be to put them back behind walls I've spent so many years erecting. Once he puts that van in gear and disappears into the horizon, I'll be alone again.

"A secret?"

I'm not even sure what I can tell him that isn't massively exhausting just to think about.

"Or it doesn't have to be a secret. Tell me about the camera you've got there?"

I thumb at the camera bag against my hip. "Isn't that kind of a cop-out?" I ask but Isamu just shrugs, so I tell him all about the brand and the film. I tell him about the specs and how it's actually a really bad camera, but something about poor quality photos makes me feel vindicated in my hazy childhood memories.

"Worth remembering," he says, laying down on the grass beside the bag of food we've been ignoring. He stretches languidly, his shirt riding above his stomach.

His dark happy trail leading below his waist band is impossible to ignore, especially against his pale skin, but I do it anyway. Instead,

I watch one of Isamu's hands thread in and out of Inu's fur, the other tugging at his ever-growing hair.

Stretched out like this, Isamu looks like something I'd want to take a picture of. His neck is smooth against the hard ridges of his veins, his muscles, his clean shave all creating shadows underneath his jaw. I am soft and rounded where Isamu's all sharp lines, and I'd need to sharpen my pencil to accurately depict its immediacy.

My fingers itch for my camera, for pencils that I normally use to paint buildings, but that's foolish because I've never taken a photo of a person. I've never drawn a person. I hate that the urge is welling up now.

Isamu sits up, all at once breaking my reverie of his angles, and begins to undo the bag, pulling out the now familiar bento boxes of food.

"I think I'd like to be something worth remembering to someone," he says, pausing his organization to look out into the park, lost in his hopes.

I press the camera to my eye and let my finger hover over the shutter. Just one photo to remember him when he's gone. To remind myself exactly why it is that I keep my emotions under check. At the last minute, I turn the camera and capture a photo of a tree above us. The last photo I took was of my mother; I can't erase that.

"What type of things do you deem are worth remembering, Johnny?" he asks, turning around to hand me a pair of white chopsticks. There's a painting of a big-eyed bear in a pink tutu on them.

"Trees," I say even though I mean desolated, barren trees that reflect my barren, desolated soul. I feel embarrassed even thinking it, but Isamu has done something odd to my emotions that I buried deeply for so long.

He smiles and hands me a bento box. There are cylindrical sushi rolls, bursting with colors; pink, green, yellow. I watch him pop one into his mouth from his own box and follow suit. It's colder than I expected, and it takes me a second to commit to the second chew as I adjust to the different textures.

"I think I told you I joined the army for my citizenship but," he starts as I swallow the sushi, invading my senses with an entirely different feeling. "Did you know Afghanistan is actually breathtaking? They don't talk about it often; how beautiful it is."

I nod to show him I'm listening as I grab a second roll. This time I can appreciate the flavors—now that I know what sort of texture to expect—and I squeeze my tongue against the roof of my mouth as I try to explode the mango flavors against the savory sauce-covered fish.

Every day, Isamu brings me food, and every day, it's easier to think about the flavors than the significance of what that could mean.

"I only got stationed in two different states before being injured," he says, "and one of those was North Carolina."

"Where was the other?" I ask. If it weren't for my dad's stations that I barely remember and my internships that I never get to enjoy, I never would have traveled out of Durham.

"Georgia," he says between grains of rice. He laughs, humor splitting his face open. "But obviously, now I'm building a van to travel around and maybe that isn't really sustainable."

He looks up at me and then sticks a single chopstick into his mouth, contemplative as he searches for the words, the reason.

"I don't belong behind a desk or in my dad's world either. I've always lived this half-in-half-out life, where I'm not smart enough to amount to anything but smart enough to pass. I'm athletic enough to get us to state championships, but not tall enough to win or make it to college. I'm too Japanese to be American and too American to be Japanese." His eyes soften, the darkness there turning to liquid onyx. "I've never belonged somewhere, not really. And then suddenly I belonged to this squad, but even that was taken away.

"Sorry. That's morbid," he says with a smile. "I don't regret joining. I just meant it's hard to feel like I don't belong anywhere. But it's all good." Isamu waves a hand. "I'm figuring it out."

He closes his box of food and reaches for Inu, where she's been eating her own bowl of food—not kibble but an actual home-cooked meal. I try to find my words as I watch him pull a tennis ball from Inu's satchel bag. Speaking is not something I'm good at, and I'm just about to pull out a secret when a guy approaches.

Isamu

Inu looks up from where she'd been sniffling at the ball in my hand at the intruder. My hands curve around the ball, metaphorical haunches raised at the hostility in his gait. The breath in my lungs is already clinging tight as I scramble upwards.

"Dogs aren't allowed here," he nearly shouts when he reaches us. "My wife is scared of them, and you're going to ruin our tour of campus if you let that attack dog keep running around."

I slam my teeth around my tongue, biting it hard as my nostrils flare while I try to remember why murking civilians is frowned upon. John's warm shoulder grazing mine dings somewhere in the back of my mind, despite my entire focus on the intruder. The potential threat has my brain tunnel visioning on nothing but the guy.

The guys fists are clenched and his face is screwed up in a disgusted look that I match tenfold.

"Sir, this a service animal, and it's within his legal right for her to be here," John says calmly.

The guy looks me up and down, as if that will suddenly make my disability visible to him. I bare my teeth at him just as a woman screams somewhere in the distance. My spine shivers with the anticipation of more intruders. They're probably just behind me.

"You don't look blind."

"Hey man, why don't you fuck off," I tell him, letting my rage spread like wildfire catching on dry leaves.

John grabs my bicep and I nearly take a swing at him in my confusion. When I turn to tell him off, anger pulses in my neck, but he's not even looking at me. Instead he's staring at the ground behind me. His eyes snap back to the man, fire hot.

"Sir, you need to go. Immediately." John raises his hands between us, trying to disarm us both.

It's a lost cause though. I'm far into seething with anger, white heat filling my vision. This guy can get fucked, because he's about to need an ambulance when I'm done with him.

"That attack dog needs to go. It's dangerous," he shouts, his beer gut that I had sized up the second he came, jiggling with ferocity.

I go to shove John aside, deciding jail time is worth breaking this guy's teeth in.

It suddenly clicks as I'm still pushing past John, that Inu has been barking with desperation the entire time, subconsciously adding to my stress.

The sky is in front of me all at once. My hands grapple as I try to grab something, but with no oxygen, I can hardly get them to respond. My breath comes out in gasping pants and there's some yelling around me. Inu fights whatever is between both of us, trying to get to me.

Inu's warm body slides under my head as the yelling continues. I'm going to die here, and this prick is going to walk away without getting socked in the face.

If I'm going to die here, someone should get my dad.

"Isamu? Isamu," John shouts as he crouches above my body, hands on my cheeks.

There isn't a way to tell him I need him to get off. I need him to not touch me but I'm too busy dying to say something. I need to die not feeling crushed. But all I feel is crushed, the residual anger wrapping around my veins, constricting them and causing my muscles to clench with the unshakeable urge to fight the world. My heart is beating rapidly; I can feel it in my neck and my feet and deep in my gut. All I want is for my body to get its shit together so I can fight this guy, but my breathing is demanding more attention.

There's no option but to release the anger and try to survive. It feels like I'm dying while my lungs flair in desperation.

"Fuck, I'm calling 911," John says, reaching for his phone.

The adrenaline in my body gives me enough strength to grip at his wrist, but white spots erupt in my vision as retribution. I know I'm squeezing the hell out of him, but John doesn't need to call anyone and cause more of a scene.

Almost fainting isn't the same as cardiac arrest. There genuinely isn't a reason for a doctor, as long as everyone stops yelling long enough for my heart to remember how to beat.

John lets his phone drop and attempts to edge his hand under my head, between Inu and I, but I let out a choking, animalistic wail, wasting precious, necessary oxygen, and thrash at him until he backs up.

I squeeze my eyes tight and try to remove myself from everything, breathing as deeply as I can. My lungs choke wetly and hot tears of strain run down my nose and lips, making everything that much worse.

Now that everything has gone silent, my brain is too loud.

Hazy memories of Afghanistan flood my senses. Smith driving

the Humvee through cities and deserts alike. Monroe meters away from me as we rucked across deadzones. Bullets engraving themselves into the wall, inches next to my face as Alvarez—third tour—cracked jokes to calm us down.

Doc.

Doc.

Doc and my fucking leg.

The screaming. Doc's, mine, everyone outside who was hit by the IED directly. Then the firefight as our position was given away while I lay butchered.

I'm not sure how much time passes with me reliving this memory. Judging on the draining light, well over an hour, but eventually the pain in my skull ebbs, and the sweat on my skin registers as it begins to cool. Soon, I'll be shivering so hard it'll be like a jackhammer; a mix of my cooled sweat and PTSD.

Closing my eyes again, I squeeze my fingers and toes, slowly moving up across my limbs, until I'm finally able to move my arm all the way to rub Inu's coarse fur from where she's still laying under my head. John is still hovering nearby, concerned eyes and hands clenched against his knees, with equal fervor as my still clenching heart.

I finally begin to sit, world spinning with nausea. The guy from earlier is gone. But John's still here.

"Are you—is there anything I can do?"

I shake my head and then nod, raising my hand silently in a request for his assistance in lifting me. John stands quickly and grabs me under the shoulder to help me up. It makes my stomach roll with discomfort to be touched right now, my skin aflame with paranoia and bullet spray.

There's still a ball and a bowl on the floor, along with a discarded meal.

"Get it," I tell Inu in a scratchy voice, pointing at the stuff.

John stands quietly beside me as Inu retrieves all the dropped objects. Once everything is back in my bag, I throw it on my back and begin to walk away.

"Where are you going?" John asks, his feet crunching on the leaves to catch up.

"Somewhere else," I grunt out.

"Can I give you a ride?" he asks, to which I don't even bother responding—there's too much noise in my head. Or the absence of noise. I can't tell the difference. "Isamu, can I please give you a ride somewhere?"

I finally turn back to him.

"I'm fine." I walk away again before thinking better and looking back to John. "Don't tell Gonzales," I tell him.

He grimaces, eyebrows still drawn down in worry. "I already did. I'm so sorry," he says, pressing fists into his eyes. "I didn't know what I was supposed to do. He told your dad who called your doctor."

Inu presses her nose into my hand, and I figure that I should probably breathe through the anger unless I actually want to go into cardiac arrest tonight.

Sighing, I start walking back to John's car. I feel like I'm in a fugue state, empty flower beds and undressing trees passing by me without notice. I'm just a zombie guided by aching limb, followed closely by a grim reaper and a man who hasn't left.

My brain is distancing me from everything that was today, and I reach with slow, unfeeling fingers for the handle of John's car. I look down at Inu who is waiting for her command and urge her up.

"Do you want to put on music?" John asks.

I look over tiredly and stare down at the cassette player in the car. It only strikes me now that we've never listened to music while he drives, only the sound of my own blabbering to fill the space between us.

"It's kind of an old car." John opens the center console, tucking his large shoulders in so I can get a full view of the tapes stuffed in there. "I've actually had to jimmy-rig a bunch of it for it to still run," he tells me with an awkward laugh. "But there's blues, you probably don't like that. Oh! There's some rap and, uh, I think I have Lana Del Rey. She's in right now, right?"

I don't think I've ever seen John try this hard to have a conversation and as we pull off campus, I see him bite his fist in discomfort.

"Uh, my favorites have star stickers. Just makes them easier to see while I'm driving," he says by way of explanation.

I start to pull one into my lap and run my fingers over the cracked plastic case. David Bowie. I can't say I ever pegged John as a Bowie fanatic, but there's a whole two stars on it. Tucking it under my leg, I grab the next starred tape, Billie Holiday—which is a name I recognize, but don't know.

"My mom was really into jazz," John says as I grab another cassette tape. "She even went as far as naming me after it." He bites his fist again.

I don't know any jazz singers named John, but it's a common enough name that I'm sure there are a lot. The new cassette is a Mitski one, and I save "hipster" under a tab of things I know about John.

The drive isn't long and we're pulling up to my apartment by the time I'm holding a Frank Ocean cassette.

John gets out of the car and then gets back in when he realizes I haven't moved.

"You know cassettes are kind of like photos in a way. Because they both work off film," he explains. "But these are the only ones I have. My dad has an old record player that we normally listen to music on. It, uhm, I've never told him, but it actually isn't the original one we had when my mom was alive. This one time, he got so drunk that when he came home, he tripped over it, and it broke—wasn't the first time he'd knocked it over. I exchanged some lunch money for the same model so he wouldn't feel bad about it."

"Seems like a lot of lunch money," I mumble down at the cassettes.

John's quiet for a second, trying to understand what I said, before finally laughing—it sounds too loud for this car. For him. "Just a year's worth, but I had been saving it under my mattress just in case. I was on voucher lunch, so it's not like it really mattered.

"Sorry, that sounds really sad. It wasn't actually that bad. My childhood was kind of fun because I had a lot of freedom. I used to spend hours at the basketball court when I'd get days off from the garage, and even a few times I'd take the bus to the mall—they still had FYE stores back then." John looks over at me and clears his throat.

"I'd walk home because sometimes there was this woman on the block playing music, just on her guitar. I'd always kind of wanted her to stop and talk to me. You know how it is when you're a kid, just wanting to be the center of attention."

If I could feel my body, if there wasn't a solid rock freezing my lips shut, I'd tell John I pay attention to him. It's all I do. Even now, in this haze of burnt ground, I pay attention.

"Anyway, one time instead of her on that corner, there was a protest. Michael Brown had just been shot in Ferguson. I'd heard about it, but something about seeing people protesting kind of rewired my brain.

"Sorry." John's eyes widen. "I'm horrible at talking. Now you probably know why I don't do it. Do you want to, uh—" he looks up at the roof, eyes frantic. "We could talk about Bob Marley?"

I get out of the car and hear John mumble behind me.

"Get busy," I tell Inu, voice quiet against the world.

Pulling a poop bag from my backpack, my hands begin to self-realize, sensitive against every touch. Everything feels like it's coming to me from beyond a screen. I'm in here, unfeeling, and everything is out there... not part of existence. Unreal and unworthy.

I can't even tell if I'm real.

I take a step forward toward my apartment and then another back, still reeling with something that tastes more like terror than anger. Gonzales is probably upstairs waiting for an explanation.

John is still standing beside the car, so I open the door to the apartment and wave him off. As soon as he's gone, I step back out.

Sometimes, there's no other option but calling in evac.

"Dad," I say into the phone clutched in my hand, voice wavering with the exhaustion I haven't let myself feel.

I smash the bag of shit against the concrete. It doesn't make me feel any better.

Chapter Ten

Isamu

猿も木から落ちる

I THOUGHT THAT sleeping in my childhood bed would bring some comfort.

It doesn't.

The house creaks with noises I'm no longer used to, and for some reason it hurts that I won't have time to relearn them before they're gone. I can hear my dad downstairs speaking to my mother in hushed Japanese. They're talking about my dad delaying his move to Japan to take care of me.

I feel like a freak. Like a half-formed version of what I used to be; the other half lost to the wind that carries the sands in the Middle East.

When you're sick, you take medicine. If you're really sick, maybe they put you on chemo or under a scalpel and pray for the best. When you lose a leg, they give you crutches and eventually a metallic stick, etched away as best they can to mimic your real leg. But when you're brain sick, there's nothing they can do about it.

Take the PTSD pills, talk about your feelings with the willingness of running a cheese grater down your heart, try not to give up. I'm not giving up. At least not permanently. Just for a few hours.

My brain has become a fever dream. Paranoid to the point that my resting heart rate screams fight or flight, all because I can't stop imaging shadows in the brightest alley. Top that with the loss of a limb that also creates heart issues, and I'm a walking disaster.

Tomorrow, instead of getting my new prosthesis like I've been waiting for so long to do, I'll be at the VA running blood tests and getting screened to see if I'm even healthy enough to go on a simple hiking trip. I should be thankful I'm even being seen. The VA normally takes months upon months to get a checkup, and maybe a smidge less for surgery.

I guess fainting enough times on base didn't only qualify me for a service dog, it also made me a model case for a crazy PTSD veteran.

Inu lifts her head from my chest and sniffs me, cold nose right against my neck. I watch her nose dig through the blankets to find my hand. I push back in acknowledgement and try to think about something else. Anything else.

But everything is stressful right now. My heart rate is still high despite my dad's best efforts, but if I think about the van, I'll be anxious it's all for nothing and if I think about John, I'll be emptied out and replaced with shame. He must think I'm a husk of a man.

The urge to scream in frustration is overpowering but my dad is downstairs, and I don't want to deal with more looks of pity today. That leaves me no other choice.

Inu shifts as I sit up in bed, tucking my head between my knee and arm, deep breaths chasing away the scream. Therapy was awkward. Being stuffed into a room with other military personnel reluctantly sharing our feelings isn't ideal. But I did learn a lot from it. We were almost all in the same boat. In fact, PTSD is actually some healthy survival mechanism that my body created to keep me safe. While I was in active combat, it made me more vigilant—prepared for anything.

The leg, on the other hand, doesn't provide any survival benefit. But it is what it is.

"Everything is fine," I whisper between my limbs. "The chances that someone is going to shoot at me are slim." I ignore my brain supplying all the ways it could happen—this is America after all. A constant voice of negativity, designed to survive a world that will never exist for me again. "And it doesn't matter that John saw me vulnerable. He either won't care and we can go back to usual or, he'll see me differently, in which case, he can fuck right off.

"There's nothing wrong with me... well there is—a lot actually—but that's okay because I've made it this far and, come what may, I can get through tomorrow. I haven't failed yet."

I breathe between my arms and knee, taking time to fill myself—lungs expanding across my chest as I try to suffocate the gross feelings still haunting my body. Eventually, I roll over and continue breathing deeply until I finally fall asleep.

Before my deployment, but still on base, I used to entertain the idea of dating a guy. I was far from home, and no longer had the fear of having the people close to me discover I was gay. The squad was easy to keep out as long as I was secretive about it. That all went out the window when I would hear the older guys talk about what it was like for them, receiving letters from their girlfriends or wives, expecting some Dear John romantic longing. They knew it wouldn't keep because the reality was, for however long they were off in Afghanistan or wherever the US had decided it needed to flash its massive metal cock with missiles bursting out the end, their girlfriends would get bored or horny or depressed. On the off chance they did wait for the guy's return, she anticipated those sweet "Military Husband Comes Home" videos, where they meet at the airport and embrace with the longing of nine or more months. Instead, most of us come back with PTSD.

Nobody wants to sleep next to that, especially when the aftermath is me quickly falling to the ground as I lose my balance, and Inu laying on my chest as I panic so hard it shakes my body, tearing me in half all over again.

Sometimes I remember the dream. Sometimes, like tonight, I don't. It doesn't matter. I still wake up stumbling out of bed, reaching for a weapon that isn't there to shoot at enemies that are ghosts in my head.

If it isn't the PTSD, it's the crippling phantom pains that keep me up at night. It seems that no matter how much mirror therapy I do, they come back after each nightmare.

Unfortunately, tonight, it's both.

I roll an antineuropathic pill in my hand—supposed to help with the phantom pains—and wonder if there's a better solution than late nights on the couch, with the television on full volume, to drown out the sound of my own screaming memories.

Inu is on the floor, lying on her back in front of the television, legs flailing in the air as she dreams of chasing squirrels. I'm glad she was able to get back to sleep after we left the shadows of my childhood room, opting for the comfort of the television in the living room. She deserves the break after the day we've had. I didn't mean to wake her up with a nightmare.

At least my dad has streaming subscriptions now and I don't have to rely on cable to muffle my thoughts. The last thing I want is some early morning sales broadcast to put me back to sleep.

The sun rises eventually, and just as it's barely peeking through the horizon, my dad comes down to start breakfast. It's always been like that with my dad, early mornings and late nights. The life of an academic is a never-ending cycle of long hours. It's not a life I would personally want for myself, preferring to lay out in the sun or hike up a mountain. But it makes him happy, and that makes me happy.

"Do you want breakfast?" he asks.

I shake my head at him and stand up, reaching for the spare crutches I keep at my dad's—I didn't want to put on my prosthesis after my nightmare.

"I'm sorry," I tell my dad, my voice shaking as I fall into his arms.

He rubs my back. "Why be sorry if you've caused no burden to me?" He pulls back and wipes my face. "That is why I am here. Shh," he says when I open my mouth. "If it weren't because of the military, you'd come here upset when you got into a fight with a boyfriend. Or you'd call me at two in the morning because your van broke down in a mountain. Maybe in another universe, you're here because you failed a college exam. That does not matter. What matters is I am here for you—big or small. You are my son and I want to be who you call when you need to be cared for again."

He pats my cheek and I watch his face scrunch-up.

"Y-you are my son. My son. I will always care for you." He wipes at his face and pats my chest. "Now, go call your mom. She cares for you too."

"Hi Mom."

There's rustling on the other end as my mom gets grandma ready for bed.

"How do you feel?"

I look down at Inu, curled up beside me with her head on my lap as we sit on a stone bench outside.

"Better," I tell her, looking up at the red trees, bamboo behind them like a natural fence in my dad's garden.

"That's all we can ask for. What happened? Have you seen your doctor yet?"

"No. It's still early here, mom. I went to the Duke Gardens with a—a friend and some asshole yelled at me for having Inu. Triggered all sorts of shit."

"You should sue him. The American way," my mom says flippantly. "Did your friend get his name?"

I laugh. She's such an advocate for me, and it's comforting even though I have to make her stand down frequently. "Nah, I think he was more stressed since he thought I was dying."

"He?" she asks, interest suddenly piqued.

"John," I start with a sad smile. "is straight."

"My other son, Jesus," she says, wrapping her Japanese accent around a Hispanic accent. "Always says it's all a, eh, constrict."

"Construct," I correct gently. "And that's gender. Gender norms?"

"Whatever. Is he cute? John?" Her accent livens up his name and I laugh at her line of questioning.

"Yeah. He's a real looker. It's kind of a problem, you know, because he's also anti-social, like you—" she makes a noise of complaint but doesn't try to fight it, "—and I always drag him to stuff to get to know him better, but maybe I'm just being annoying."

"You're just like your father. He always took me out for drinks with our coworkers."

I laugh as she tells the stories of their youth, and I try not to lose hope that John might not want anything to do with me now.

John

When my dad's contract with the military ended, he debated getting a storage unit for the furniture we had accumulated at our on-base housing, since it wouldn't fit in the trailer. In the end, he had to call a buddy to sell it instead because he was too drunk to take care of it. He didn't give me a say in it, despite how much of it was mine.

It's a complicated feeling, seeing my dad once as the alcoholic screw up, spewing his guts across the living room, to the now frail but kind man he is today. I want to have hope in him, but I'm too scared. I just can't trust him; can't see past the man that made me feel like an unlovable piece of discarded trash.

But now I'm at the same storage units we once almost had, chasing another complicated feeling.

"Hey," I say, knocking on the side of the unit door. It's unnecessary as Inu has already alerted Isamu to my presence, but it feels rude not to.

He sighs. Maybe I shouldn't have come.

"Listen," Isamu starts, turning around, eyes darting away from mine. "About last time." He stands up fully, which is still short comparatively.

"We don't have to..." He's kept all my pieces. I can keep his just as well.

He laughs, a little wet sounding, and thrusts out a bag. "Token of my appreciation. If you'll have it, I guess."

"Of course," I tell him with ease. "It doesn't change anything."

I take the bag, expecting the typical food, only to find a cassette tape: Judas Priest.

"Not sure how you feel about heavy metal but, uh, thought you might..."

Getting food from Isamu is one thing—payment for the van. But this isn't just a gift from an employer. This is a thought-out piece of him—heavy metal—with a piece of me. It's kind, considerate and wrecking me just a little.

I grin and run my thumb over the label. "Yeah. I might."

Isamu is smiling back at me when I look up, and I feel my lungs seize. This is a horrible idea—by my brain, by my heart, by whatever chemical my brain is releasing that causes Isamu's smile to affect me.

"You should see if you can get a better sound system, especially since you're hitting the road in a few months," I say, pointing at the van, begging him to look away so I can keep pretending I'm not affected by him.

Isamu's face blanks in confusion and he looks back at the van. "Oh! Yeah, of course. The van."

"The van," I repeat, because the van is the reason he still doesn't know I'm gay. Because it's one thing giving him secrets, and it's another thing to hope he'll hold onto them long enough for me to understand why I've told him anything in the first place. The van is the reason he doesn't know the rest. He's leaving. He has no reason to know.

Isamu takes the respirator I hand to him, and our fingers get tangled in the straps. His elegant fingers pull away quickly from where they graze my hand, but too late. He thrusts the mask on quickly to cover the blushing of his cheeks, and I turn on the sander to cover the pounding of my heart.

Hospitals don't bother me. Whenever I meet people that say hospitals make them anxious, it makes me feel exhausted. Exhausted of them.

I've been to the hospital more times than I care to count. I've grown immune to the effects it has. When I was ten, my aunt rushed me here, thinking my mom wasn't DOA. She was, and there was no one to say goodbye to. In my childhood, I lounged around with a camera in my hands, my thoughts on homework I hadn't gotten to, while I waited for my dad to get stitches for his most recent drunken fall. Now, I come for all my doctor's visits.

"John Love," the nurse calls from the door with a smile.

Despite having to come here every three months, I doubt she remembers me. There are people in the lobby who have obviously just begun coming here; layered in baggy clothes, hair cut, or wigs placed haphazardly as they begin their journeys of self-discovery. Their faces are pinched in fear and embarrassment.

It's nothing to look down on, but it makes me wish I were a braver man like Isamu. He'd be able to easily reach out to the person I sat beside and have a long chat with them, easing their tension and giving them hope.

My childhood would've been different if I had met Isamu when we were still in high school. I can just imagine him reaching out to me, asking me to join the basketball team, despite my once slim frame covered in baggy hoodies. I wonder if he'd be disappointed to learn I'm not allowed to play basketball.

I wonder if he'd be disappointed if he knew why.

"Hi John," Doctor Shelby says when they step into the room. "How are you?"

"Uh, I'm good," I say, because it's mostly true.

"Any changes?" they ask, sitting in front of the computer. I watch them go over my checklist, looking over what the nurse had written.

"My face is less oily and I think I'm about done with puberty. Just leveling out I'd say."

When I first started visiting this clinic at eighteen, these sessions were long. I had come with low expectations, knowing that hormone replacement therapy takes some people months or even years for anything to change, but I'd been excited for every little thing. With no one in my life to share it with, I shared it with my doctor and nurses, secretly begging someone to care.

"Today, I got my first chest hair," I'd say, thinking of that little nub of black hair, still pin straight until it had the chance to grow further and curl.

"My voice is getting deeper, don't you think?" And the doctors and nurses would say yes, even though it just sounded like a female who was losing their voice.

"I'm scheduled for top surgery. I've been saving up." But I had to reschedule when my dad needed money for the lot.

"Everyone on campus thinks I'm a guy," I'd say excitedly, and the nurse would smile back and say, "No, John. They know you're a guy."

Eventually, I bit the bullet and gave this part of myself to Aaliyah. She was probably the best choice, since she's never looked at me differently or asked for more of my past.

I had a theory that my dad just accepted it because he was too drunk to remember if he had a son or daughter, but in his sobriety, I've realized he just didn't care that I am transgender.

"That's good," Dr. Shelby says, referring to my second puberty. "Your last blood tests came back fine so there's no reason to be concerned about your cholesterol. Do you have any questions for me before I send you your next three months' supply?"

I hesitate, pulling at my knuckles that have always felt smaller than they should be.

"What happens if HRT is banned in North Carolina?" I ask, but I know the answer. I've researched it. It's why the rally is so important. I just need to hear them say it.

It's easier to be honest with my doctors than with anyone else. They've been nothing but kind to me, but that's in part because I had heard so many horror stories that I researched the best queer facilities. It helps that Dr. Shelby is nonbinary; it makes me feel safer.

They sigh and pinch their lips. "John, we're doing everything to make sure that doesn't happen. But if it does, there are options of going over state lines to get your prescription or seeing an online doctor and getting it shipped to a different state."

I nod, knowing that's basically code for "you're fucked" because all the surrounding states are red states. If North Carolina goes down, a swing state, the others are already down too, and there goes my life-saving medication.

It's a war on drugs all over again but instead of targeting people of color, the government is coming for the queers. "Protecting children" they say, or they tack on a label of mental illness.

Those people in the waiting room should be excited for their transition, not scared of how the world will react. I was lucky to be socially transitioned as a child, and then have the ability to go through medical transitioning in the middle of my senior year, and go to college where no one knew me. No one from my graduating class except me attended Duke; not many get accepted. It wasn't meant to be a secret I was trans, but for the first time in my life, I felt so comfortable. And eventually it felt like it was too late to say anything.

When I still didn't trust my dad, Aaliyah took care of me after my top surgery, but that's it.

People would only look at me differently. See me as less than a man.

I keep it to myself unless someone has a good reason to know.

"I'm sorry, John," Dr. Shelby says sympathetically.

"I know."

Chapter Eleven

Isamu

恋とせきとは隠されぬ。

I SNATCH THE sandwich baggie Gonzales tosses me, feeling it squelch sadly in my hand. The forest around us is wet with autumn rain and the crows caw sporadically, watching our progress through the small trail. I lean, putting more pressure on my biological leg, and open the bag. My brand new prosthetic leg underneath me is silky black, that isn't exactly necessary for its hiking benefits, but still looks badass.

Stability. Structure. Independence.

That's the idea anyway.

I'm glad I was able to get the new one for hiking, but I'm worried I'll have to refit it a few times before it's actually ready for the great outdoors. I pace up the trail as I eat—ignoring that the action reminds me of my dad—but my prosthesis locks all the way before bending. If it didn't, I would fall.

Gonzales gets behind me, caressing my arms as if I would fall. It's all for show, we've been hiking for an hour now and, though I'm ache-y, nothing has gone amiss.

"Bro," I complain through a laugh. "I can literally feel your dick. Back up."

He scoots closer and I elbow him through a laugh. "Since when are you cuddle-shy?" he asks once he finally lets go.

I shove the sandwich baggie into my pack. This is similar enough of a movement to a squat, but there is too little trust for me to believe that my knee will lock correctly.

"Is John stealing my boy's heart?" he jokes as he pours water into a portable doggie bowl for Inu.

"John?" I ask, feeling a little too transparent.

"I guess I kind of got the vibe that you guys would be good together."

I brush my hands against my pants, ridding myself of all the crumbs, and stare at Gonzales in confusion.

"John's not gay," I tell him.

Gonzales nods slowly, pursing his lips as he snaps the lid shut on his water bottle. "Right," he clicks his tongue. "I guess I just assumed since, uh, the rally. Yeah? But, you know what they say about assuming." He laughs awkwardly, eyes trained on the trees instead of me.

I take the bottle out of his hands, but his eyes stay focused elsewhere. I would rather think of my prosthesis tripping me up than this conversation anyway.

"What rally?" I ask, taking a few jogging steps. My prosthesis drags a little against the ground and I adjust my lift.

"A—Aaliyah's rally." He waves his hand. "Just... a thing she's doing. Queer."

"It's queer?" I ask. "What do you know?"

"Uh, not much," Gonzales says.

I turn from him and take a step, side-to-side to figuring out how to comfortably lift my prosthesis. I tell myself it's just the ski lunges I do to workout, but my body isn't processing with my brain, fear keeping us from connecting correctly.

Gonzales doesn't return to me. Instead, he walks over to his bag propped against a rock and pulls out his phone.

"Is John gay?" I shout, willing my heart to not speed up. My watch is always storing data for the doctors, and I'm even more on edge because of it. I have to present it all to the doctor next week in hopes that they clear me to travel.

"No! Sorry, I don't know why I assumed," he says, not even looking up from his phone.

"Right," I mumble, disappointed. "Ready?"

Gonzales jogs back and motions me to keep walking, phone still gripped in his other hand. I'm only just deciding to ignore his odd behavior as the phone begins to ring. He leaves me gawking and answers the call. It takes him a while, but when he comes back, he's awkwardly rotating the phone in one hand.

"Uh, how do you feel about John though?"

I roll my eyes and start hiking again. "Why's it matter? I'm just going to leave soon and I'll probably never see him again." My watch starts beeping slowly, and I shut it off before holding my hand out to Inu who snuffles at me but doesn't give me her paw.

Gonzales waits as I finish my deep breathing before he speaks. "That's not true. You'll come back and see me. Besides, he and I are friends now."

"Why did you assume he's gay?" I ask, climb up the trail.

Gonzales sighs and walks beside me. "Just a dumb mistake. I don't know his sexuality but, uh, maybe you could ask."

I watch as the trees shake under the wind and Inu's ears flop with each step. Her eyes, ever so soulful, look up at me.

"If he hasn't told me by now, it's because he doesn't want me to know."

"Listen," Gonzales starts. "When you had just come back from

Afghanistan and were still in that *pinche* hospital bed, you had these eyes, man." He runs a hand over his face and sighs. "It felt like you weren't there with us. Trying to talk to you was like wading through this fog. I, honestly, thought we'd never get you back. Everything made you jump or lash out. Man, I've never told you this, but I cried. I cried so hard every night those first few weeks.

"I'm still here and so are you, but I swear, if you don't give yourself the opportunity to really be here, I'm going to kick your ass."

Before I can think further on it, Gonzales is slapping my ass before running away.

"No more feelings though. What if you have to run from bears?" he calls back.

"That's not—that's not even what you're supposed to do with bears," I argue as I shakily try to catch up.

John

Gonzales stares at me guiltily. I watch Aaliyah a few feet away, distracting Isamu by explaining the poster route for the rally.

"Why doesn't he know?" Gonzales asks, voice barely above a whisper and yet still somehow yelling.

I avoid his eyes by fidgeting with my camera, pretending to adjust settings Polaroids don't even have.

"It never came up. But you didn't tell him, right?" I peek over at Aaliyah and Isamu. She makes a face, letting me know she's running out of bullshit to stall him with.

"No. Put my whole foot in my mouth, but no. He bought that I had no clue if you were or weren't. Why doesn't he know?" Gonzales asks again.

I shrug and let go of my camera. Gonzales leans forward.

"But you like him," he says, enunciating each word slowly.

Isamu is leaving soon. No matter how many times he blushes after our hands touch when passing a screwdriver back and forth, or how many home-cooked meals he brings me, or how he listens to every worry—every doubt—he is still building an escape route. And I'm helping him.

"Doesn't matter." He'll leave. He'll be gone, and everything that I spilled to him will be lying on the floor of that storage unit, covered in flakes of his own stories.

Isamu looks back and smiles. It isn't one of his cheesier ones—the showy, flashy ones he gives Gonzales when he wins an argument. It isn't the impish, mischievous one that he flashes at Aaliyah before teasing her. It's the one he gives me in the storage unit when we're alone, and I've got my hand wrapped around his to show him how to fix the wiring in the van, just in case it malfunctions while he's on the road.

Do I smile at him that way?

"So, you drew these?" Isamu asks when Aaliyah releases him, holding up a flyer.

"Yep. Is Inu coming with us?" I ask him, noting she still doesn't have her service vest on.

He shakes his head and runs a hand through his hair—it's spilling over his severe cheek bones. "No, but she hates being alone, so I was thinking we could drop her off at my dad's office."

I rock back on my heels and gesture for him to lead the way, too embarrassed to admit I know his dad. It might annoy him to learn that his dad talks about him during class sometimes. There's even a big grinning photo of Isamu on Professor Miura's desk, one that I had forgotten about until we're standing in his office.

Professor Miura stands from his desk, glasses askew, and hair messy from his weathered fingers running through it. "John," he shouts in surprise.

Isamu looks back at me, bemused. "Wow, both I and your grand-dog take the backburner when he's here, I guess."

Professor Miura walks over and claps his son on the shoulder before bringing him in for a tight hug. "I am always excited to see my family. I just hadn't realized you were making it bigger," he says with a crooked grin.

It's only when he looks over at me that I realize what he meant, but before I can say anything, Isamu beats me to the punch.

He speaks in rapid Japanese, face clutched in his hands as it burns hot. Professor Miura responds back, laughing jovially before patting his son on the back and turning to me.

"I apologize for the mistake. I should've known better, my son has never brought home any man, much less such a respectable one."

I laugh, embarrassed, as Isamu hands over Inu's leash with more words I can't understand.

"Let's go, John," he says, the redness in his cheeks now running down his neck. "And you, no more talking," Isamu says to his dad before shutting the door firmly.

We stand in silence outside of the door, Isamu's back to me where I'm still holding the stack of flyers.

"He says more embarrassing things than that about you in class, if that makes you feel better," I tell him with a grin he can't see.

"Motherfucker," Isamu complains before turning around to face me. "Let's pretend he and his big mouth don't exist."

He snatches a flyer from my hand and tapes it to his dad's door with a firm slap. We're technically supposed to ask Professors first if we can do that, but I guess Isamu's dad doesn't count.

Isamu stalks off and I rush to catch up to him, grin still teasing against my lips.

"Don't be all pouty," I tease. "He's better than my dad."

Isamu grunts and leads us to the middle of the Quad. There are cafeterias and student centers where we have to hang these up so we get to work, mindlessly chatting about Isamu's doctor and his new prosthesis.

As the pile diminishes, I can't help but feel Isamu's fingers linger on mine more and more. I let him hold the flyers just for a break from his touch. It's too much.

The last flyer goes up on a lamp post, soon to be covered in ads for roommates for off-campus seniors, study groups, and the occasional student band.

"Have you ever had a boyfriend?" Isamu asks, admiring his handy work. The fact that he's facing away from me does nothing to hide the redness on the tips of his ears.

If Gonzales weren't all the way on West Campus right now, the ugly stepchild of East Campus where the freshman live, I'd fight him. I am in no way ready for this conversation. I don't even know why Isamu thinks he is, if he's so ready to leave.

"Nope," I answer, rubbing a hand over my mouth as I try to bottle up everything else. The "I can't ask you to stay," the "I wish you wouldn't leave because I have actual feelings for you no matter how hard I try to ignore them," the "I can't stand the thought of only sleeping with you just to watch you walk away," and the "I'm trans."

"Really?" He asks with a sly laugh, finally turning around. "Someone as attractive as you?"

I bite the inside of my cheek. *Please don't do this*, I beg internally. Externally, I say, "Nah, never dated anyone. Just too hard to please."

This isn't a conversation we should be having. He's leaving. He doesn't know I'm trans—had no reason to until now. He's leaving. I'm too busy with school.

He's leaving.

He waits.

"Isamu," I start, pinching the bridge of my nose. "What are you doing?"

He frowns and rolls out his shoulder. "So you are gay?"

His voice comes out quiet and I realize he's angry.

His anger has never been directed at me. Hours of work in a cramped van, sweat dripping off us as he learns an entirely new skill, and he's never once been angry at me. But now, he's silently seething.

I let his anger sit as we stand there, no flyers to distract us, until he finally lets out a breath and I brace for the onslaught.

"Sorry, you didn't owe it to me to say anything. It just kind of hurts my feelings that you didn't," he says, hands on his hips as he turns back to our handywork.

"What?" I ask, hands wrapping around the camera around my neck as I block my heart off.

He looks over at me, exasperated. "It just hurts, man. I know you're private, and you're entitled to that, but I thought we were," he gestures between us. "I thought we were friends at least."

I rub at my eyes, willing the image of Isamu's sad face out of them.

"We are," I start. "We are friends," I finish with more certainty. "I just didn't want . . . things to change. Expectations."

He bites his lip, anger flashing a bit, hands clenching against his biceps as he crosses his arms. "Damn, Johnny, rejected before I could even get out of the gate."

I groan, frustration mounting. "No. I just—I meant—the van. I'm working on your van and—" I gesture, not wanting to tell him I can't handle another person in my life not being there for me. But I also can't stand the thought of him sacrificing his dreams for whatever this may be. If there is a "this".

Isamu takes two steps away from me, then two returning steps back before repeating the process. "That isn't what I meant. This didn't go down how I wanted it to." He squeezes his eyes shut.

He opens them and takes one last step forward.

"I like you, John."

I wait, expecting a "but". None comes so I wait a little longer, sorting through everything that I was purposefully burying.

Isamu's face slowly falls into uncertainty the longer I wait.

There's bile rising in my stomach as I try to push down everything—all that I've kept secret from him. The way it feels when he smiles, the way I feel when he fondly takes care of Inu—of me—the way it feels when his fingers graze mine. I bury it because he's leaving, and I've already been left by so many people that I can't stand one more.

"John?" he prompts, reaching for one of my hands still wrapped around my camera.

I step backward and we both watch as the cord of my camera snaps and my camera tumbles to the ground.

"John, I'm so—" Isamu starts.

"I can't do this," is all I can say, making the decision to be the first one to walk away.

Chapter Twelve

Isamu

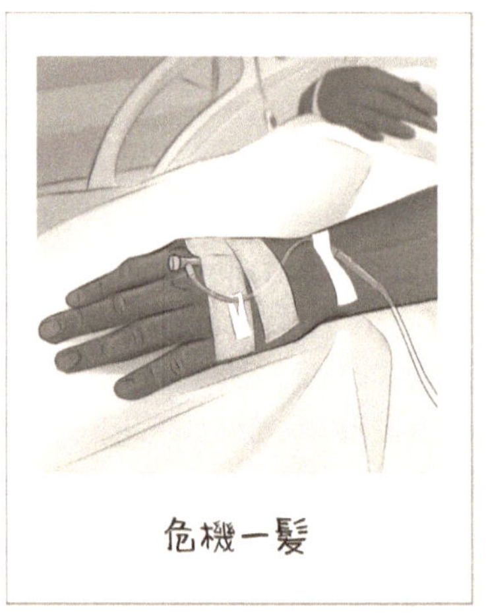

THE TREES HAVE LOST all their leaves. I used to climb up high into the trees and tuck myself away against the leaves, scared that if my parents saw my tears from unbridled typical teenage angst, they'd worry.

I guiltily fall back into my childhood habit as I wallow.

It was beyond stupid of me to confess to John. All my patience has been thrown out the window on a whim and a broken camera strap. But he's more than just a whim. If I had only had the chance to get everything out, maybe he would've understood. Now, it's too late.

My mother and I have always been obsessed with dramas. Doesn't matter the kind: Japanese, Spanish, Korean, American—we watched it all. But I'll never forget the day she held my face in her hands as we watched a soap opera.

"Isamu, listen to me. If a girl ever says 'no,' you listen to her and walk away. End of conversation, no questions asked. Do you understand?"

I had understood then, looking at the severity in my mother's eyes and I understand now. John said his two cents before I could, and that's that. Now, I only have this deep, unforgiving forest to comfort me and a van that I can only hope he'll still work on.

Not like there is much left. Spring is a few months away, but last night, I went ahead and reserved a campground in Death Valley National Park, starting the second finals are over. My old man and Gonzales will be upset that I'm missing another Christmas, but there's barely any work left on the van and California doesn't get cold enough in the winter to snow. At least Death Valley doesn't.

"Son," my dad calls from below me.

I was hoping that by ignoring the opening and closing of the back-door, he'd miss me hanging out high in the trees above his garden.

"Your phone is ringing. Do you want me to answer it?"

I look down, barely making out that the call has already been answered, but I can't see the name. Waving him off, I turn back to the sky. Soon, every night I'll look up and see nothing but stars.

"John, he is in a tree and he is not coming down. Should I take a message?"

My fingers grapple into the hard bark as I nearly fall.

"Dad. Stop, shut up! Don't say anything else. I'm coming down." I scramble down the tree as fast as I can, my movement less than ideal with my prosthesis.

He hands me the phone, and I grimace as I look down at John's name flashing across my screen.

"Hey, what's up?" I ask, clearing my throat.

My dad stares at me and I shoo him away.

"I'm on my way to the storage unit. Just wanted to let you know since that's what's scheduled," John says, his voice monotone like it was at the beginning. It makes my entire body ache with loss.

"Of course, yeah. I'm, uh, there right now," I lie, which he obviously knows because he just talked to my dad about me being in a tree. "Or, uh, yeah. I'll meet you there." I hang up before I have to hear any more of his monotone voice.

Rushing into the house, I call for Inu. She's already there, vest in mouth. "Good girl," I say, scratching under her chin.

She noses at my palm and I groan as I check my watch. "It's not that bad," I tell her, now slowing down to give my heart a chance to catch up. I'm forced to take my dad's car since we're running late, and there's no easy way to get to the storage unit from his house.

By the time I get there, John is already standing outside, hand wrapped around his backpack strap, staring blankly at the ground. Despite the cold, the sky starts to sprinkle rain on us.

"Shit, sorry man," I say in a rush, unlocking the storage unit. "I know how much you hate having your time wasted. I just didn't think you'd come after... sorry." I run my hand through my hair and grimace as I pull out a twig, now wet from the rain.

"We had an agreement," he says, walking into the storage unit. "Besides. This is the last day you'll need me."

I stop putting on Inu's vest, having forgotten it earlier in my rush. "What do you mean?" I ask.

He doesn't look up as he drops his bag to the ground and pulls his jacket off. Unsurprisingly, his arms don't look any less appealing just because he rejected me.

"After the countertop is installed, all that's left is décor. You don't need me for that, Isamu." He hops into the van, quickly getting measurements that I've seen him do a million times already. "It's better for me anyway since I have finals coming up, and the protest."

"Right," I say, voice lost in the sound of John snapping the measuring tape back.

The silence between us builds as we install the countertop. It builds like a tension that sears through my heart and my gut, taking me apart bit by bit, only broken by the sound of heavy rain falling on the storage unit. I'm nearly trembling with the need to say something—anything—but every thought is aborted before I can put them into words. Before I ever get the chance, the new countertop is shiny and installed.

"John," I start, feeling the impending end like a gunshot. I won't ask him out again, but I just want to try and be his friend again before I go.

He looks up at me, eyes pleading—for what, I'm not sure. Maybe he wants me to shut up. I'm probably supposed to shut up. Before I've decided what to do, John's phone starts to ring.

His brow furrows as he pulls it out of his pocket and jumps out of the van.

"Hello?"

I can't hear what the voice says on the other end of the line, but I get out of the van just in time to watch John's uncaring mask fall from his face, eyes widening and mouth dropping in unbridled fear.

"What hospital?" he asks, voice hardened.

John hangs up, face set in determination and turns away.

"John?" I call, but he doesn't turn, instead walking steadily into the pouring rain. "Is your dad okay?" I ask. He's the only one I could think of that would be in the hospital, but I thought he didn't drink anymore.

John gets into his rust bucket and turns the key, met with nothing but spluttering. John turns it again. More spluttering. He slaps the steering wheel and begins to yell.

"John," I shout, tearing open his door, my fingers slipping on the handle's wetness, but he's still screaming, tears running down his cheeks. I grab his bicep and haul him out of the car.

"It's fucking dead, Isamu," he sobs. "It's never died. Not once. It's my dad's. It's my dad's car."

I'm still manhandling him into my own dad's car, the rain pelting onto us as he keeps crying, fists closed tightly against his eyes, digging in so hard that I just know he's seeing spots. I can't tell him it's okay because I don't know that it is, and I can't tell him his dad is fine because he might not be. But I would do anything to make it so.

Inu is attentively standing beside me, and I open the door for her to hop in before going to the driver's seat.

"John," I say but he isn't listening, still sobbing uncontrollably beside me. "John," I try again, grabbing his thigh. "What hospital?" I really hope it's a hospital and not a morgue.

"Duke. By the VA," he says, breath gasping.

I throw the car into reverse and peel out, water splashing out below my tires. I'm good in emergencies. Emergencies are the only language that feels normal to me after Afghanistan, and I smoothly put us on the freeway and through the tiny roads until we're at the hospital, John's sobbing the only thing keeping me focused.

When I throw the car into park, I expect John to rush out of my car, but he's frozen in fear.

"What if he's already dead?" he sobs. "Why does everyone keep fucking leaving?"

I try not to think of how I'm leaving him. I try not to think of his camera that's in my bag. I only think of what I can do for John in this moment and realize there isn't anything but just being here for him.

I wrap my arms around him, clinging tightly as my heart sobs with him. Burying my face in his shoulder, I let his tears join the rain on my shirt until he's ready.

John

My dad laughs from where he's hooked up to a bunch of tubes, hand in mine as I lay with my head on his bed. We've been here for fourteen hours.

Isamu is curled up in a corner sitting on a chair, mouth wide open as he snores in what's possibly the least comfortable position in the world. His snoring rivals the thunder that's been rumbling throughout the night.

"And so, I told your ma that we should name you Tyler because I thought it was a perfectly acceptable name for a girl. But, no. I'm never right. We named you—well, you know what we named you. Bet you wished we named you Tyler, huh?"

I yawn and shake my head at my dad's antics. "I probably still would've changed my name, pa." There would've been too many female memories tied into that name.

He laughs and then coughs, trying to hide that he's clutching at his stomach.

"Don't talk about that right now anyway," I tell him, eyes flitting over to Isamu, but if he's faking his sleep, he's the best actor I've ever met.

My dad catches my gaze and looks over at Isamu. "You know, I have eyes." He waggles a finger at me. "That boy is a looker."

I roll my eyes at him, annoyed that he can be so jovial when he's dying this week. I run my hands over his sunken cheeks and let my tears fall down my face. He wipes them away like he's been doing all night, regret painted into every wrinkle.

"I'm sorry, John."

"Don't," I say, stopping him. "Not yet. You've still got time." I press my lips into his boney hands.

My dad sighs, laying his head back against the pillow as Isamu's phone begins to ring. He wakes with a yell and the phone hits the floor, but Inu is already on her feet, head caressing Isamu's hands as he gathers his bearings.

"That would've been nice," my dad comments as we both stare at Isamu, thinking of all my dad's PTSD.

"Wouldn't have gotten approved with all the drinking. I looked into it once," I tell him.

He grunts as Isamu finally picks up the phone from the ground, eyes carefully avoiding us. "W'ass up?" he asks, voice thick with sleep. "Mmm, yeah. I texted you the room number."

Isamu hangs up and puts his head back against the wall as he rubs Inu's head.

"Is that Aaliyah?" I ask.

"Mhm, she brought Gonzales," Isamu responds, rubbing sleep from his eyes.

I cringe and he shrugs in apology. "She's your friend, man. Blame her for not being able to keep her mouth shut."

Internally, I smile at Isamu's morning crankiness. Externally, I roll my eyes as he stands, taking Inu with him.

"You should go," my dad says. "I'll still be here when you come back."

I hum in thought and squeeze his hand before standing.

The scene outside my dad's room is not ideal. Gonzales looks like he's barely holding onto sanity. Aaliyah's eyes are clearly bloodshot from crying, and she's carrying a bag of dog food. They're both wet from the rain.

"Aaliyah, I said I needed food for a week, not a whole month," Isamu teases, impish smile on his face as he reaches for the bag.

"You're staying the whole time?" I ask, shocked.

Isamu looks back, surprised to see me, before turning away, not fast enough so I don't see his blush. Before I can comment though, Aaliyah is wrapping her arms around me.

"John," she wails against my shoulder, covered in grime, sweat and Isamu's face where he dug in hours ago. I can still feel the heat from it.

"I had no clue. I should've been there for you," Aaliyah continues as we cling to each other.

I shake my head and cling tighter, knowing it's my fault that she didn't know. But now she's here and her arms embrace me, keeping everything I'm feeling from spilling out. I've never thought of sharing this with her, too worried about her judgment to stomach it. She may not get along with her family, but her dad's a politician who is successful and capable. My dad's dying because he couldn't get his shit together.

My dad and I's relationship may not be rock solid, but the only person who can judge him is me. I've been letting that fear of judgment keep me from this. This intimacy with my best friend where I don't have to be alone. I don't have to face the pain of what's happening to my father alone.

Gonzales comes over and puts his hand on Aaliyah's shoulder. She pulls away from me slightly, still keeping her hands on my shoulders.

"Sorry," he says. "Aaliyah was in no state to drive. We brought your clothes and the textbooks you asked for. How is he?" Gonzales asks.

"He's going to die," I say, tasting the truth on my tongue and finding it bitter and cold. I turn to Aaliyah and say, "You should go say hi to him. He knows a lot about you. I'm going to change." I motion to the clothes.

When I come back to my dad's room, they're crowded around him and, for a second, I'm scared he's outed me as they laugh at something he says.

"But let me tell you, John was a force of nature. You know, he used to get into a lot of fights at school and everything."

"Our John?" Aaliyah exclaims, grabbing me and wrapping her hands around my forearm. "He's a softy."

Gonzales nods. "I can believe it. I thought he was going to swing on me that day I went and asked him to work on Isamu's van."

I lean closer to Aaliyah.

"Where's Isamu?"

She smiles at me. "No clue. Why don't you go look for him?"

I roll my eyes and wander out of the room. There's a lot of things I should say to Isamu. Thanks would be a start, but when I find him in the bathroom, there's dog food spilled all over the floor. I rush over to help him.

Inu watches us fumble the torn open bag, her leash in her mouth as she looks up at us sweetly. I might have pet her if my hands weren't so full.

"Thanks," Isamu says with an awkward laugh as he wrangles the bag and begins to pick up dog food.

He's been doing his best not to be awkward, but I can hear all the moments he's hesitated to exist near me. Like stop-start traffic on the highway to the beach, but he's too scared to move forward and I can't blame him. In fact, I'm glad he's at a full stop. I can't handle trying to parse through what his being here means.

We look at each other, the moment heavy with the things we haven't said, but my dad's in the other room. Isamu is something I can deal with... after.

"Thanks for being here," I manage before I turn and hold the door for him to exit.

He gives me a tight-lipped smile and leads the way.

"I hope I'm not overstepping," he says, barely discernible as he moves away from me. "Figured you want someone to be here for you. But now that Aaliyah is here, I can go home. If you want that, I mean. I'm okay with whatever."

I grunt and keep following silently, not sure how I feel about what I want.

"We have class soon," Aaliyah says sadly as I come in, and she presses her arm against mine. She's warm against the chill of the hospital. "I can call out though, I just don't know if you want space or company." She looks up at me questioningly.

Now that she knows, I realize I want nothing more than her comfort—nothing more than her nails scratching at my skull while she holds me. But finals are coming up and she needs to study, not sit around here and watch the inevitable.

"It's fine. I'd like to spend some time with him," I tell her, giving her a hug.

Gonzales, surprisingly, also gives me a hug. His bulky arms, rivalling mine, embrace me as he squeezes all my pain out for just a few seconds.

"I should walk them out," Isamu says, awkwardly pointing over his shoulder.

"See you in a bit," I tell him, making my decision.

He nods and turns away as I return to my father. His stomach is swollen underneath the blankets which are piled high on him. I look away, grabbing at his thin hand instead, thinking of all the meals he had skipped.

If I had been more insistent on it, he wouldn't be here so soon. If I had been braver as a child, less self-absorbed in my own survival, I could've saved him from the bottle. If he hadn't been such a piece of shit.

"Isamu seems like a good . . ." my dad starts, a smirk on his lips.

"Friend," I finish for him, heart heavy with a confession that'll never come.

He laughs, then coughs. "Friend? A handsome boy like that? Ain't no friend of mine ever look at me like that."

I roll my eyes but he reaches his other hand forward, and I oblige.

"John, you gotta know when to take a good thing. Him coming here and staying the whole night with your smelly, dying dad is a good thing. Being there for—" his voice cracks and he coughs away the thickness. "He's taking care of you, and that's all a dad can hope for. He's got—he's got love in his heart for you, more than enough to be there for you in your time of need."

I pull my hand away from him, as the anger that's been welling in me for eleven years starts to tip over the edge.

"Why could you never do that for me?" Tears pool in my eyes, heavier now because it's been so long since crying came naturally.

"Oh, John."

"No," I say, shaking my head angrily. "No. You don't get to do that," I spit out. "Why did you never love me? What about me was never enough to make you stay?"

He sighs and looks down at the sheets where his fingers pull at non-existent strings. He looks away from me. Away from my anger.

"When I lost your mom, my brain just sort of . . . stopped. Something deep in me snapped. This'll just sound like an excuse and I—I guess it is, but I lost so many friends in Afghanistan. Before that, I lost my own ma to cancer and my pa to meth. I watched friends get shot by cops. I held my baby sister as she bled out.

"Y'all were everything to me. The reason God made me suffer everything before. Y'all were—" he sobs deeply, making my heart spasm against my own tears that choke up my throat. "Y'all were my light at the end of the tunnel. When your ma died, I was so scared you were gonna be next. I just didn't wanna be here for it. So, I pretended you were already gone, hoping it would save me from the pain when you were."

My teeth dig into my knuckles as I hold in my screams, sobs of frustration, years of an absentee father.

The cold hard realization that I'm his carbon copy.

"I'm still here, dad. I've always been here, and you were so damn scared that you took everything from me when mom died."

Unwilling to see any more pain on his face, I rush out of the room. The hospital is loud with expectation, machines beeping and patients' tears. This isn't the first time I've been here, but this is the last time I'll be here with my dad.

Thinking of it, the last words I said now feel like a plague, tearing apart all the years I've kept my head down and taken care of my dad. But there's too many years of resentment and I feel myself flip flopping between hatred and longing.

It's how Isamu finds me in the stairwell a little while later.

I look up at the sound of clacking claws and the soft scrape of his shoes. He plops beside me, not even complaining that he probably scoured the entire hospital for me.

"Hey," he says, keeping a fair distance away from me.

It makes me wish I hadn't told him no to his confession. Everything makes me wish I hadn't told him no. I wanted to say I liked him too. I'm just stupid. And scared. Which makes me a lot more like my father than I ever wanted to be.

I guess it wasn't the bottle I should've been scared of.

"Want a secret?" I ask.

"Only if you want to give it."

"I—I used to wish my dad would die. Or disappear. It was so hard taking care of him, and I thought, maybe, I had suffered enough that someone would adopt me and actually take care of me for once. Sometimes I just wanted him to die so he could suffer instead."

"Johnny." Isamu reaches out and grabs me by the shoulder.

It's all I need to break, and I turn to him, burying my face against his neck.

"I don't want him to die. I don't want to be alone and—and he's finally starting to be a good dad and I just fucking told him he's a piece of shit and now he's going to die thinking that's how I feel."

Isamu rubs my back and Inu noses between us, sensing anxiety from the pile of our limbs. I pet her as she noses against my belly, surprised by the softness of her downy fur beneath the coarseness.

"Thanks for being here," I say, reluctantly picking my head up from Isamu's shoulder and unwinding my hands from Inu's fur.

A nurse comes into the room right after we do, and she smiles kindly at all of us. "How nice that y'all have stayed here so long," she exclaims happily. "But I'm going to have to ask anyone that isn't kin to leave."

The doctor comes in behind her and I flinch, fearing the deadline has gotten shorter.

Isamu squeezes my hand before leaving.

I plop on the chair, bones like gelatin as fear fills me corner to corner.

"We have a few more questions for you," the doctor starts as the nurse begins to inspect his vitals. "There has been absolutely no drug or alcohol use since your diagnosis, is that correct?"

I shove my knuckles into my mouth, ready to hear the reason he's in here so soon is because he's been secretly drinking.

"No, doctor. Honestly, I haven't. My boy here can attest to it," he says, eyes wide.

The doctor looks at me and I pull my knuckles from my mouth. "As far as I know, other than his prescribed medication, he hasn't been taking anything or drinking since the cirrhosis diagnosis."

The doctor nods and then looks at the nurse who nods.

"Well. Here's the bad news for someone else and good news for you. There was a pile up last night on I-85 because of the rain. Because of the advancement of your cirrhosis and because of the pile up, we've got a liver for you, Mr. Love."

A noise comes out of my throat, of shock, surprise, elation, and my dad reaches out, grabbing me tightly beside him.

"A liver?" he asks, disbelief in his voice.

"Yep, and you're compatible. We'll have the anesthesiologist in here shortly."

Chapter Thirteen

John

AALIYAH DROPS BY after class, sitting beside me outside of the surgery unit while Isamu takes Inu on a walk. Although, Isamu was so antsy, I think the walk was more for him.

"I can't believe they found a donor," she says, nails scratching against my skull. "I think we should redo your jewelry."

"I'm not doing trans colors," I tell her. She's already asked me to do them for the rally.

"Not what I meant. Just new bling."

"Next you'll want me to get synthetic hair like you," I complain.

She grins and flips her braids over her shoulder dramatically. "Martin said he liked it."

"Hate that you call my dad by his first name. Y'all should've never met, but he loves you by default. Let's not talk about him right now." Somewhere beyond those doors, he's being cut open and dissected. He'll be on more medicine for life just to keep the liver from being rejected.

"Let's talk about the rally then. I'm excited. Just a few more days, baby!"

I groan.

"What's with the attitude?" she asks, flicking my forehead.

Sitting up, I put my head on my hands. "I don't know, Liyah. Does it mean anything? Like, we protested in Black Lives Matter, and yet here we are still being shot left and right and lynched while we protested in California. It's like it doesn't mean anything. Politicians don't listen to us."

I look over at Aaliyah. Her face is stone, jaw grit so tight that I'm worried her teeth might crack.

"What?" I snap, annoyed.

"John Love, you have got to be fucking kidding me. I'm not yelling because I am not getting kicked out of this hospital while your dad's in there, but so help me God, I would yell so hard. Do you think for one second that just because something is hard, we should give up?" She thrusts a finger into my chest.

"That's not—"

"No, John. Shut the fuck up and listen. Did Harriet Tubman—"

I groan.

"Did. Harriet. Fucking. Tubman. Give up? Did she say, 'oh, it's really hard to free my brothers and sisters from these white slavers. I'll just call it good and quits.' Did she?"

I shake my head.

"No. She went back and back and back, over and over again, John Love. Did Martin Luther King Jr. give up when he was threatened and attacked? Damn John, they had to assassinate him to keep him down."

"I know—"

"No, John. You don't know." She slaps me across the shoulder, chiding. "Rosa Parks? Shirley Chisholm? Bayard Rustin?"

"You're right."

"Damn straight," she says, getting in my face. "Shit is hard, John. Your dad is in there and maybe your stressing is why you're so stupid today, but don't you dare look in the face of our ancestors and say, 'shit's hard'. Of course shit's hard—we're Black. But if Harriet Tubman, small little Black Queen she was, can face down crackers and dogs while running with babies and our folks across the river, you can nut up and fight for our trans siblings the way Martha P. Johnson did."

She huffs out a breath and turns from me, crossing her legs delicately.

"Are you done?" she snaps.

"Yeah. I'm sorry."

"Nuh-uh. Do better next time. Piss me the fuck off, John." Despite her words, she leans in and hugs me. "Listen, even if you're feeling scared and down and like you can't do it, I swear I will underground railroad that lifesaving hormone therapy to people. Just expect me to rope you into it."

I laugh and wipe at my dripping nose—forgetting whatever thought I had about crying. This week has been a lot. "Wouldn't have it any other way, Liyah."

"Stupid ass," she chastises one last time.

"Is, uh—am I intruding?" Isamu asks.

"Not at all," Aaliyah tells him, smiling. "Come on, he should be out here soon."

Isamu sticks out like the first orange leaf in autumn as he stands in my dad's kitchen. It might be the bright orange Ralph Lauren polo against the dark woods of the cabinets, but it's also the knife kit he brought with him, shiny and silver, that he's using to cut carrots while I study on the couch, Inu's head on my knee.

My dad's snoring can be heard from his room, recovering from being torn open and replaced. Gutted from his mistakes and from mine.

Isamu has been here for it all. Helping me carry my dad in from the car, cooking him soupy meals that he can actually stomach, and then making another for me while I study until it feels like my eyes will bleed.

Don't leave, I want to say, but the van is done, nothing but cushions and utensils left to buy, and I catch him on his phone late at night scrolling through bedsheets and sending emails for backcountry passes to National Parks. He's leaving.

I just can't let him leave without saying something. I won't make the same mistakes my pa did.

"Isamu."

"Hmm?" He looks up from where he's dropped carrots into the blender.

My dad's obsessed with carrot soup and anything else high in Vitamin D, a food group he had to avoid when he had cirrhosis. Which is a concept I'm still getting used to.

"Rally's next week," I say, because it's easier to think about than the finals I've been too frazzled to study for. Isamu is too close and my dad is finally healthy; finals seem like the least important thing now.

"You excited?" His hand is still on the blender top, and I motion for him to go ahead, just to give myself a second to get my thoughts together.

"More nervous," I say once the blender's done its thing. "Kind of nerve wracking to protest something that affects me so much, you know?" I look away from him, back down to my open textbook on the coffee table that was once only used for beer cans. "It's really important that people like me have access to their hormones."

I'm still not looking but I hear the second Isamu stops mixing the soup, his ladle going still against the pot. It's a heavy second, then two. Inu rises from the couch and goes into the kitchen. Then it starts up again, Isamu picking up the conversation as if there was never a pause.

"I'm sure a lot of people will turn up. It's a life-or-death medical necessity for people, so it's bullshit in the first place that it's being taken away." He scoffs. "Protect children, my ass."

Isamu's back is to me, shoulder muscles visible against his shirt as he cooks. I don't want to lose this view. I don't want to lose him. But I have to make sure.

"You got that I'm transgender, right?" I ask, voice tight as I fight waves of fears and insecurities.

Isamu looks back at me, a grin on his face. "Yeah, Johnny. I got that. Just kind of figured you didn't want to make a big deal of it."

My dad's fresh out of the hospital and I've kept the secret so close to my chest for so long. Isamu's been chipping away at my walls bit by bit, and it's all crumbling down as I feel my face fall apart.

"Woah, hey—hey. Shit." Isamu fumbles the pot off the stove and comes over to me, dropping to a crouch between the couch and the coffee table as he puts his hand on my knee. "Johnny? What's wrong?"

"I'm just scared," I say, teeth gritted as I try to keep from falling apart.

"Fuck, dude. Hey, come on. Don't look so down. There's nothing... it doesn't change anything for me." Isamu rubs my knees, brows furrowed above wide, pleading eyes.

"You, uh, do you still like me?" I look at him, trying to mask my face so he doesn't see the weight of the question. I don't want him to see how much his answer means and how destroyed I'm going to feel if he rejects me.

I just don't want him to walk away from me.

Isamu

A laugh escapes from my throat like a gasp and I sit my butt down on the floor, letting my head rest on John's bare knee. A knee that I've been dying to put my hands on since I saw him this morning, walking out with a bedhead mess of locs and ratty basketball shorts.

My face is warm against him and I'm discovering that there's even a limit to *my* bravery as I look at the floor as opposed to John.

"John," I start, feeling my heart tighten in my chest before letting it all go in a rush of acceptance. He's already rejected me once and here I am on the floor in front of him. I'd always come back for John. "My face is tingly against your leg. Every time I'm near you, it feels like I can't breathe, like Inu should be barking because I'm about to faint. When I touch you, I'm—I'm absolutely charged with it."

Fingers against skin, pinpricks that send electric shock through my body as I long for more. I want so much of John that he devours me. I would happily bury myself against John and never need for more.

"Just because you didn't get the memo that you were a guy at first, doesn't change that. I mean," I laugh self-deprecatingly. "You rejected me, and I still dream about how your hands feel in my hair, how you would look against my pillow. I feel like I'm floating any-time I imagine you in the van with me, miles from here and all our problems. We'd be below the stars with a cassette tape playing in the background and my fancy cooking skills to impress you.

"I hope this isn't scaring you off, but I am way past being trapped in your orbit. I am gladly obsessed with your eyes and your arms—God, your arms—and the way you've given me so much about you. I feel so honored to know you, John. Everything. So, I guess to me it isn't a big deal that you're transgender because I'm still gay and you're still the man that I—" I pause, hands clinging to his knee as I bite my lip with all the pressure erupting from my chest. "And I'm seriously falling for you, John. Or, I already have, if we're trading secrets again."

John pulls me up from his knee and wipes at my face, tacky with sweat from the stress.

"You're onto something with keeping secrets. I'm embarrassing myself," I say, stupid as I drown in his dark brown eyes.

"You're not," he says, leaning forward.

His lips taste like mint and like the open roads of freedom and like home. His lips are soft and everything all at once. I chase them when he pulls back laughing.

"Wait," he says, pulling back again. His eyes follow my tongue as I go to taste the memory of his lips against my own. "Uhm, date. You want to go on a date?"

My cheeks are probably red enough to illuminate the room as I nod, lean in again, and chase those lips just a little more. And then more. Until everything is John and the way he smells like the trees and engine grease, and the way his hands feel against my back and chest and the way his jaw feels under my teeth.

We only stop when the sounds of his dad waking up give us pause.

"I should—the soup," I say, pulling my hand from the back of John's neck.

He leans forward and steals one more kiss. "Yeah. The soup," he whispers, his crooked teeth shining behind his wide smile.

Chapter Fourteen

John

以心伝心

"I'M SORRY FOR BUGGING you earlier about that guy," my dad mumbles sleepily in his bed.

I tuck his blanket up to his chin, making sure the pillows that keep him elevated are right in the middle.

"Don't worry about that," I tell him, reaching for his blanket-covered hand. "I want you to know that I'm really glad you're here. I know—" I cough into my shoulder and look away, annoyed that I can feel so many feelings in such quick succession. "I know I said some things when we were in the hospital. But I need you to know—I need you to really know that I'm glad you're here."

He looks up at me with wide eyes and smiles. "I know I haven't been a good dad, John, but I'm glad you're my kid. I'm proud of you even though I get that I don't have any stake in your upbringing."

I pat his hand and walk out of his room. There isn't much more to say. I don't know if I'll ever be able to look at my dad and feel the same way about him that Isamu feels about his dad. But I am glad he's still here. I'm glad that he's trying.

The rest of the mobile is dark, except for the living room where I can see Isamu's light from the couch. He's been sleeping here just in case my dad needs something, but I imagine the couch isn't a comfy place.

When I come over, he has his prosthesis thrown off the side and his other foot tapping along to a beat only he can hear. I had originally thought he took off his prosthesis every day when he got home—assuming it was just as uncomfortable as a binder—but he only really takes it off to shower.

"Hey," I say, wanting to run my hands through his messy hair but still a little unsure.

He smiles up at me and reaches his hand out, loosely grabbing my wrist.

"Aww, come to keep me and Inu company on the couch?" he teases.

I lean in slowly and he eagerly lifts himself to meet his lips against mine.

"You don't have to sleep on the couch if you don't want to. My bed is big enough," I tell him, finally running my hand through his dark wiry hair.

He perks up and grins, scrambling off the couch to follow me, leaving Inu behind where she's sleeping on her back—legs in the air as she runs in her dreams. My legs feel a little wobbly, nerves of having Isamu in my bed making my entire body feel like a spark plug.

My childhood bedroom isn't much. There aren't photos tacked to the walls; instead they're shoved in a box underneath my bed and its plain sheet. Nonetheless, Isamu looks at everything as if I've given him a gift, hands running over a pile of notebooks on my desk.

"This is exactly what I pictured," he says with a grin, turning over a few old cassette tapes.

"Boring?" I ask, suddenly worried now that I've let Isamu in, he won't like what he finds.

"Nah," he says with a shake of his head. He turns around and smiles at me, thumbing at a cassette tape. "If I didn't know you the way I do, maybe I wouldn't see it. But you're all over this room." He takes a step toward me and puts a cassette tape in my hand.

It's one from my childhood that my mom made for me. I run my thumb over the crossed-out name that was once written on it in my mom's handwriting, only the "J" of my deadname still visible, followed by my own scratchy middle school handwriting.

"My mom made me this. We were driving back from base to Durham."

Isamu wraps his hand around mine where I hold onto the tape.

"You want to tell me about her?" he asks, but I'm already shaking my head.

I put the cassette on my bedside table—just a bright red milk crate—and sit on my bed, still clinging to Isamu's hands. He follows me, stepping between my legs.

"I think I've done enough emotions for the rest of my life," I say, leaning my forehead against his stomach. "Last secret?"

He laughs and intertwines his fingers with mine—his fingers are thinner than mine, and I feel the warm sensation of gender affirmation as mine encompass his. It's a rare thing for trans men, so I cherish it even harder.

"I sure hope not. There's too much about you that I don't know yet," he complains sweetly.

I drag my hand leisurely over the back of his leg. When he shivers, I go to pull it away, but he hastily grabs my hand with the one that was scratching my head and puts it back.

"I'm really nervous to get undressed in front of you," I say, quietly, tightening my hand around him.

"Well, you don't have to," he says, matching the whisper of my voice.

"Not like that," I say, shaking my head against his stomach. "Do you ever... wish we'd met before?"

He snorts and continues to rub his stubby nails against my head. "Yeah, this would've been nice to have before. I mean . . . I had Gonzales and my dad, but I was still lonely."

I bite my lip, annoyed that the route I've taken to avoid speaking about my mom is the same route that dredges up old feelings. "I was really lonely, Isa." My chest hurts and my eyes protest as the torrential downpour of emotions overwhelms me.

"But," I continue. "The biggest thing is that I just wish I would've had someone to share everything with. Like all the transitioning stuff." A cold laugh escapes my throat and I pull away from Isamu. "Maybe that's dumb, but it feels like all my milestones went unseen."

Isamu doesn't let me put distance between us and crowds into me even more, which is a feat when we were already nothing but points of contact.

Slowly, he falls into bed beside me and presses his lips sweetly against mine.

"So, tell me about them."

I laugh, a little embarrassed, and grab his hand pressing it to my chin. My stubble there makes me feel just like any other guy. It gives me confidence I never thought I'd have. "I used to just be this baby face."

He moves his hand to cradle my cheek and presses a kiss to my scruff. "How long ago did you start taking testosterone?"

"About as soon as I turned eighteen and I didn't need to rely on my dad to approve anything," I say against his lips that have veered to mine.

"What else?" he asks, hands snaking up under my shirt, resting on my waist. It makes me laugh with the memory of how much I hated that part of myself. Hip dysphoria was an issue I only cured by burying myself in textbooks.

"Well, you know. It's puberty, so a whole slew of things you probably don't care about."

He smiles and noses against my shirt. "Come on. Tell me your embarrassing second puberty stories and I'll tell you mine."

"When I had top surgery, I got so sweaty that Aaliyah had to put baby powder underneath my surgery vest so I wouldn't get sweat acne."

He laughs and leans back to look at me. "Can I?" he asks, tugging lightly at my shirt.

"The scars aren't visible. I got them tattooed over. Black skin isn't as forgiving about scars," I explain before lifting my shirt over my head.

He runs a hand across my tattoos, suddenly distracted by them and forgetting the scars all together. Maybe he never really cared about the scars at all.

"I used to get awkward boners," I tell him as the feeling of his fingertips across my pecs sends tingles across my skin. The nerves there will never be the same, but I feel like it was a fair trade off to get rid of my chest tissue.

He chokes out a laugh. "Mhm, same. Don't think that's exclusive to you."

"At least mine weren't visible," I say with a smirk.

He looks up at me and rolls his eyes. "Well, aren't we lucky. What else?"

I take a deep breath, suddenly uncomfortable. Every part of me looks and smells like a man except one. The one some people can't seem to get over. I have to push at the pit in my throat to say it to Isamu—to trust him enough to not care.

"When I got my first packer, I just stood in this room for hours in nothing but boxers staring at myself and, ha, like doing this happy dance, I guess?" It wasn't the first time I had packed, but it was the first time I'd used anything but socks. My first official dick that I ordered off some gender affirming website that guaranteed discreet packaging. It didn't cost much, but I still had to take some money off my dad's disability check for it.

Isamu's eyes don't drift from my chest, but I can sense he's fighting the urge to look. "Do you want to know my secret?" he asks with an embarrassed grin.

What I really want is his immediate validation. "Sure," I say tentatively.

"I spent all day googling transgender affirming things, because I'm fucking stupid. Anyway, I ended up on a website for packers," he says with a giggle. "Did you know that there are some that are like thousands of dollars and custom made?"

I give him a bemused look and he splutters.

"Wait, like not that you have to get one or anything," he says quickly, holding up his hands in defense. "I literally do not care if you have a meta or phalloplasty or literally no changes since how you were born—"

"How far down the rabbit hole did you go?" I ask, surprised he knows all these terms for different bottom surgeries I've only ever dreamt of with my lack of funds.

He grins sheepishly. "Uh, I watched vlogs and spent a lot of time on the Reddit threads for FTM folks."

"You could've just asked me about that stuff." But I still feel giddy that he's chosen to like—love—every part of me.

Isamu snuggles against me, wrapping his leg around me and burying his face between my pecs. I had no doubt he'd be such a clingy person, but I feel all the discomfort melt off me. This is nice and I hadn't expected that his clinginess would be so welcome.

"I know that," he starts, lips brushing against my skin. "That's what Reddit said, but I didn't want to go into this totally blind."

I laugh and wrap him in my arms. "Well, if you want an anatomy lesson," I tease.

He snorts and slaps my shoulder lightly. "Fuck, Johnny. What, are you in high school?"

"Is it working?" I ask.

He groans and presses his hips against mine. "Yes."

Isamu

John isn't in bed the next morning when I wake up in a haze. I call for Inu who trots in excitedly as if I didn't sexile her the night before.

"Do you want—" Martin asks, following in after her.

I squawk and pull the blanket up to my chest, face bursting with red that probably matches the rising sun.

"Stop that. Nothing I ain't seen from my time in the army," he says, waving a hand. "You want breakfast?"

"Should you be out of bed?" I ask, about to scramble out and suddenly remembering I'm naked and unfortunately unwashed from last night's endeavors. "Where's John?"

Martin shuffles away. I hop out of bed and throw on my briefs and a pair of John's sweatpants.

"He's in class, and I'm grown. I can get out of bed if I say so," Martin calls from the kitchen.

I look down at my prosthesis as I cuff John's too-long sweats over them. "Yeah? Think they can give you another liver if you don't listen to your doctor and get an infection?" John's shirt is also too big, but I pull it over my head anyway before going into the kitchen.

I lean against the doorway and lift up my pants leg to show Martin my prosthesis. "I know a thing or two about healing."

He grumbles at me in a generally John way.

"Listen, it sucks being stuck without mobility. Trust me. I fucking get that. But it's going to suck more if you strain yourself and John has to deal with you being sick again." I drop my pant leg and smile as Martin walks past me to the bedroom.

"Fine. But you're making breakfast," he says, hobbling back into bed.

I roll my eyes fondly, grabbing an ice pack from the freezer before bringing it to him.

"Here. I'm sure you're regretting that." He probably regrets it even more since John flushed his painkillers after the first day. Those things are bad enough for people without addiction issues, and the last thing Martin needs is to begin another addiction.

"Hey," he calls as I turn to leave. "My boy, you gonna treat him nice, you here?"

I have to stifle my smirk. If he had a shotgun, I'm sure he'd be holding it right now. I can just picture Martin, if I were still a teenager in high school picking John up for prom or something, sitting on the front porch, cleaning the shotgun for effect.

"Of course, better than you could," I tease, knowing that since he's a vet, he's going to understand the humor with no bars.

"Them eggs better be good, boy, or I'm gonna take back my approval," he calls, laughing as I retreat back. "Where were you?"

"Fort Bragg," I tell him. "Although, they changed it to Fort Liberty the year I was injured."

"82nd?" he asks. I peek my head out of the kitchen to make sure he's still in bed.

"Yes, sir," I reply once I see he's still in bed. "What about you?"

"Fort Bliss," he tells me and I cringe at my own question, realizing I actually don't know what division he was in, but knowing it was probably something with tanks.

I put the eggs back in the fridge—he shouldn't be having foods high in salt or fat so soon after the transplant—and start to toast some whole grain bread. The cantaloupe is perfect, and I put some chili powder on top, wishing it was mango like Gonzales eats so frequently. I pop a slice into my mouth and groan. It isn't the same, but it's still good.

Martin accepts the plate gratefully and then looks down at the cantaloupe with confusion. "What is this?"

"Chili powder. Don't tell me I'm seasoning better than you are?"

He frowns looking at the cantaloupe slice in his hand. "If I could throw right now, I'd hit you with one of these. Why don't you go bother John? He's probably just about done with his final now anyway."

My stomach clenches as I remember why John wasn't in bed this morning. We stayed up so late last night and now he's probably suffering through his final. I'll make sure to stop and get him coffee on my way.

Inu and I loiter around campus, sleepy students passing by us. As we wait for John, I pass her a treat for sitting so calmly beside me.

"Oh, thank fuck," he says, grabbing the coffee out of my hand. "Why didn't you remind me I had a final today?" He downs the entire coffee and leads me to the library.

"Can I take Inu in there?" I ask, clutching his hand. I also should go back to my apartment at some point and check in with Gonzales. I don't want to be the type of friend who disappears off the planet when I suddenly have a . . . a not-boyfriend but more than a friend.

John pauses and looks down at her. She's in her vest, but I still tell him he can pet her. John arches his eyebrow at me and shakes his head.

"Yeah, not falling into your bad training. I see how many scraps of food you try giving her while you cook."

I grumble a complaint that he ignores.

"She should be fine, but I guess that's up to you if you want to risk someone asking?"

I shrug. "Can't stay scared forever," I say, feeling like I'll be scared forever anyway.

The library is packed with last-minute crammers, but I spy a head of curly hair attached to a set of broad shoulders I'd recognize anywhere.

"Gonzales!" I shout.

John immediately lets go of my hand, turning away from me just as four people look up at me with anger on their faces.

I hold my hand in apology and walk over to Gonzales.

"Your boyfriend really seems to have your back," he teases as I sit across from him. I look down at his papers splayed out and push them neatly aside so I can lay my head down.

"I'm already embarrassed," I say with a groan. "I don't think I've stopped embarrassing myself since we kissed."

Gonzales leans forward and grins. "Oh?"

Aaliyah chooses that moment to sit beside me. "God, that final was awful."

"Sorry *amor*, but you're gonna need to hold that complaint a few more seconds because my boy here had his first kiss," Gonzales jokes just as John pulls up a chair beside him, looking at me with shock.

"No!" Someone shushes me, and I hold up my leash as if I can sick Inu on them. They turn away, properly reprimanded and I turn back to John. "No, that was not my first kiss or my first—" I blush. "Fucking shit, Gonzales."

He laughs quietly. "It's a running joke we have. Don't worry about it," he placates John. "So, now that John has timed his entrance perfectly, tell me about that exam, Aaliyah."

Aaliyah shakes her head at us and starts to tell Gonzales about it, but John looks across the table at me and presses his foot against mine. I can only tell because of the vibrations all the way in my thigh, but he's pressed against the wrong one.

"Other one," I whisper at him, as to not draw more attention to me or disturb Aaliyah's diatribe about electronics or some shit.

He gives me a confused look and then it dawns on him.

"Sorry," he says, readjusting.

This time I press my foot against his, then turn to listen to Aaliyah even though I don't understand a word she's saying. Being surrounded by college students makes my brain have a moment where it thinks, *do I want this*, quickly followed by a, *no, definitely not*. Look at Gonzales's eyebags. But when I look across at John, I wonder if maybe there is something I'm missing out on. Maybe I don't know if I want to go across the country anymore. Maybe my home is still right here in Durham.

Chapter Fourteen

John

ISAMU'S HANDS are ice cold against my sides. I juggle my coffee above his head so I can keep myself warm against the early morning chill.

"It's so early," he grumbles against my neck.

Inu's pressed against my side, and I use my other hand to scratch her forehead. I watch as Aaliyah comes down from her dorm room, cardboard in hand. She's bundled against the Carolina winter that isn't even cold enough to put snow on the ground.

"He gets it," she says, nodding toward Isamu. "You're a menace to society for only wearing that."

I shrug in my flimsy zip-up. The testosterone I inject into my body once a week keeps me warm enough, and winter is the only time that I feel any semblance of relief from the humidity. That and I don't really own a lot of warmer clothes. The warmer something keeps you, the more expensive it is.

"He's also bitching that it's too early," I tell her, trying unsuccessfully to unravel myself from Isamu.

He immediately unglues himself from me and looks up with wide eyes. "Wouldn't want to be anywhere else though."

I roll my eyes at him, only because the sentimentality tugs at my heart in a way I'm only starting to grow used to. Too many years of shutting out my emotions is making this transition a test of my nerves and Isamu's patience.

"*Oralé*, party's here!" I turn at the sound of Gonzales's voice, just as a few students begin to pour out from the dorms, too early to be students taking their finals. Gonzales looks chipper and bright-eyed which is for the best, else he'd get taken down by the storm that is Aaliyah on game day.

As more people join us, Aaliyah begins to give her instructions, lining us up as far across campus as we reach. Gonzales follows her, carrying supplies and handing out posters. A member of the club that I recognize, but don't remember the name of, comes up to me with little tubes of face paint in their hands.

"Wassup, John. You want a trans flag on your cheek?" they ask, holding up the tubes.

"Uh..."

"I'll get one," Isamu says with a smile, stepping up toward them.

"Sweet," they say, voice still crackly from the early morning. "Just your cheek?"

"Deck me out," he says as another student comes up with shirts.

Aaliyah had told us to wear all black, but the student is wearing a trans flag on their shirt and carries more in their hands. I watch in awe as Isamu asks for one. He takes Inu's vest off and puts it in his backpack, telling her she's off duty, before putting the shirt on her.

After the student with the shirts walks away, Isamu leans against me, taking pressure off his residual limb, minding the paint now covering his face. He leans against me silently, absorbing my body heat and waiting for students to wake up for breakfast and exams. The silence eats away at me until I can't hold it in.

"Now you're going to look like you're the trans one," I tell him, my voice hushed against the other whispered conversations going on around us.

He shrugs. "I don't mind."

I take a sip from my mug, slip my hand into the side pocket on Isamu's bag, grabbing the thermos. My hands shake slightly as I top off my mug—a pride flag one from a local bookstore in Chapel Hill. I let the heat of the coffee fill me, calming the cold in my heart placed there by fear.

"Is it still wet?" I ask, gesturing at the face paint.

Isamu sticks a finger against it, and it comes back light blue. "Guess so."

I grab his chin, mindful of the wetness there, and quickly press my recently shaved cheek against his.

"There. Now I've got some too," I tell him, turning away.

He bumps his poster against me just as the first student slips out of the dorms, unaware of the protests until he sees us. We're a silent, looming line of students wearing all black. A reflection of the bleak future that transgender folks everywhere face.

I down my coffee quickly and set my mug at my feet before grabbing the poster I designed ages ago.

I was afraid I'd put too much detail into it: the faces of Black queer folks like Marsha P. Johnson, Bayard Rustin, James Baldwin, Barbara Jordan all surrounding the words, "Nearly Half (49%) of Black Trans Folks Attempt Suicide", only made better by Isamu's own "Trans Rights are Human Rights". My fears are all for nothing because as students come out, they all slow down, caught by the flashes of color on my poster and intimidated by the long line of students, standing silently through their walk across campus—an unavoidable wall of reality.

This is my reality that they're forced to face. It may be a small campus, but they will not go another day pretending this doesn't exist. That this doesn't affect them, as they see their friends silently stand in a line, protesting for their friends, family, strangers, or themselves.

Even though I've been to protests, organized them, shouted at the world, I've never worn the trans flag on my body, too afraid of how it may change how people see me or how they listen. There's nothing wrong with living in stealth, but I've never felt so seen as I do with Isamu in silent support beside me.

We've been standing for a few hours when someone comes up to relieve me for my final. I tuck my poster board under my arm as I lean down to grab my backpack.

"You don't have to stay," I tell Isamu, concerned for the hours he's spent on his prosthesis.

"Nah, I don't, but I'm going to anyway," he says with a grin.

I glance at the guy who's taken my place and back at Isamu.

"Alright. Well, wish me luck," I say, reluctant to take a step back.

He pouts at me and I lean in to steal a kiss from him.

"Luck, Johnny boy."

Walking toward my final makes me appreciate the intimidation of the protest a lot more. Hundreds of students shadow my entire walk to class, silently staring straight ahead as they wear black. It's disquieting and impossible to ignore. There are bystander students taking photos of the displays around campus, news crews covering the protest shoved in places they won't disturb exams, and the silent faces of stoney support—unyielding to the world of bigotry.

Isamu

I shove the heat pack under the driver's seat when I spot John. His face is stoic like always, but even he can't hide the lightness in his eyes, the ease of his gaze. More than anything, I hope today has shown him he doesn't have to be so alone. His struggle isn't for only him to bear.

I also really hope that by the end of this date, he doesn't dump me before we've even really started dating.

"Look at this bad boy," he says, opening the back instead of climbing into the front.

"Admire your handy work later. I've got a date to take you on," I call out, desperately trying to keep him from spotting the dinner I spent the day before prepping and then this evening finishing.

He laughs and closes the door before finally getting into the passenger seat.

Inu hops off the bed in the back to investigate him, and I watch proudly as he pets her. It feels like acceptance. It feels like I may be about to throw this all out and I don't know if that's what I want.

"Where are we—"

"It's a secret," I say, cutting him off.

He laughs and fiddles with the stereo system, easily syncing to my phone that instantaneously plays the angst heavy metal I thrive on. I cringe but he leaves it on, evaluating the sound as BABYMET-AL doxxes me.

"Not what I imagined."

"What did you imagine?" I ask, taking the ramp for the highway.

He hums and I fight the urge to take my eyes off the road. "Something peppier. Like sunshine music."

"What does sunshine music even entail?" I ask, laughing.

I listen to his explanation, shoving my phone under my leg as I think of all the music I have that fits that very description.

When I first met John, talking to him was like pulling stitches from his mouth. Every word seemed painful to him, every secret a battle to fight. Now he talks without a pause for breath; willing to share his thoughts without hesitation. I've dug my way into his heart with bleeding hands and desperation, but what he doesn't know is that he's torn mine open with ease.

If he tells me not to go on this trip, I won't. If he tells me to sell the van and instead builds us a house, I'd do it without thought. I'm a fool because I've spent hours on the phone with my army buddies telling them they're stupid for this exact thing. But I get it.

This man beside me is worth it. There wasn't a reason to stay in North Carolina anymore but suddenly it's here. I only wish I could take him with me. I want to see the world but he's becoming my world. He's splitting me in two directions.

My anxieties don't disappear as I pull up to Eno River, lit up by the moon, but they do ease as a smile graces John's face.

"A picnic?"

"Well, it's cold so I figured an indoor picnic. Christening of the van, if you will."

I ignore his smirk and the blush on my cheeks, getting up and going to the living space. I busy my hands by pulling out the meal, but it's hard to ignore John in such a cramped space. He towers over me, taking dishes and setting up the dining area, still tucked away to give the van more room.

"Ramen?" he asks as I flick off the overhead lights, leaving us only illuminated by the mood lighting we set up.

"Authentic," I tell him, pulling out the wine glasses for the sparkling juice. It feels braggy to tell him the tonkotsu broth soaked overnight and the bones were tediously selected to provide the best flavors. It's not the way I normally make ramen, preferring the quicker recipes with premade broth or just buying them from street vendors. But I'm going out of my way to impress him.

I suddenly feel nervous as I sit across from him, worried that he won't like it. But when he takes his first bite, he barely comes back up until the bowl is clear, broth and all.

"You have to teach me to cook someday," he says, leaning back against the booth that doubles as a couch.

I lean my head against him, pushing my half-eaten bowl away. "Mmm, I will. Once I get back."

I'm glad I didn't eat more because my gut bubbles with anxiety—to the point I'm afraid the broth will make a reappearance.

He laughs and kisses my head, which only adds to the pain in my heart. "Yeah? I'm sure we can find some time in my busy schedule to cook before spring."

"Spring?" I ask, basking in his arms that are slowly wrapping around my waist. Soon, they'll be gone.

"Sure. That's when you leave, right? Once it gets warmer."

I grab his hand, tracing the callouses he has from working on cars all day.

"I leave after finals," I say in a whisper, barely audible if it weren't for my head against his chest.

He stiffens against me and I almost cry out when he shifts away from me.

"I'm sorry. I know long distance probably isn't what you were looking forward to and I'm more than willing to shift the dates to stay a little longer," I look over at him; his brows are furrowed, and I plow forward. "Or just cancel it all together. I'm sure I could sell the van and get my money back—maybe even get a profit—"

"Long distance?" he asks, cutting me off.

I stare at him, realizing he's confused. "Is that… is that not… oh shit, you don't want that."

"That's not what I'm saying," he says, clutching his shoulder and scooting away. "Hold on." He takes a deep breath. "You should go. Even if it's sooner than I expected. And I want you to go, if that's what you want. I'm just scared you won't want to come back, but… I don't want to live like my dad—looking back in eleven years and realizing I missed out on something good because I was too scared to even try."

I press my face into his palm. "I will always come back, John."

His thumb rubs my cheek. "Yeah, I'm trying to learn that," he says with a sigh. "Long distance isn't ideal but, honestly, you've seen how busy I am. I'd be a terrible boyfriend right now anyway."

"Boyfriend," I repeat. "Will you be mine?" I ask, pulling my face away from him so I can look into his eyes.

His eyes are a clearer brown than they normally are, lit with joy. "Yeah."

His lips are chapped from the cold, but I press against him with the same neediness I always do, eager to be closer. Eager for everything John will give me.

"Wait," I say, pulling away despite everything within me arguing against it. "I had this idea. How would you feel about coming with me during holiday break? Then just flying back?"

He smiles but shakes his head. "My dad just got out of the hospital and plane tickets are expensive."

"Oh. That's fair. Well—" I'm interrupted as he leans in and kisses me.

"Hmm?" he hums against my lips as he pulls me in.

"Uh…" I pull back again. "Shenandoah. It's near DC, you've done your internships there, right? I could go there this summer. I'll spend the weekends with you and go back to Shenandoah during the week, so you don't have to entertain me during the work week."

He steals another kiss and another. "Whatever works, Isa. Just live your dream and come back to me."

His hands encircle my waist and I forget whatever it is that we were talking about as soon as he smirks. "So, about that christening?"

"Are you sure?" I ask John, clutching the Polaroid camera tentatively. The last time I held it, I broke it.

John sighs playfully and hits the power button. "Are you really going to tell me you're patient enough to wait for your phone photos to be ready?"

I shake my head and he frowns in mock annoyance. "I didn't think so."

Grinning, I lean up to kiss the annoyance off his face before running off.

I have to crouch to take a photo with my dad, both of us competing to smile the largest.

"Be safe," he says, holding my face as the photo develops. "And don't forget to eat, or call your mom."

I laugh. "Sure, sure. I'll call you too, Old Man."

He hugs me. "I love you."

"Love you too."

Gonzales is looking at the van when I get to him. "I'll take a gap semester or something before I start my master's, and we can travel."

"I'd love that, man," I tell him, pulling him against me. "Now, before we get sentimental, say cheese."

I get to Aaliyah last, making sure to give her an extra big hug.

"Hey, I want you to know I seriously appreciate what you're doing for John."

She waves me off, her nails still painted blue, pink, and white. "You're kidding. A Christmas where I get to spend it away from my parents and with John's dad instead? A dream come true."

I give her another hug, just to be sure.

"Okay. We should probably head out if we want to get to the campsite," I say.

John hoists his bag onto his shoulder but keeps talking to his dad, probably lecturing him about taking his meds and eating every meal.

"You know how to change a tire?" my dad asks.

I look at John. "Yeah, no problem."

"I said you, not your boyfriend."

I blush and give my dad a hug before going to John. I don't rush him, but he watches me amble over and says his final goodbyes to his own dad.

"Ready?" I ask him, excited to get on the road.

"Uh..." He fumbles with his bag and pulls out a sturdier camera. "Actually, I want to remember this moment," he says, tone heavy.

I let his Polaroid hang by my neck as I reach out for John, grabbing his forearm delicately. "Yeah. I think that's a great idea."

"A, uh, nice clear shot. Of all of us. Things are good, yeah?"

He looks uncertain. A little afraid, a little hopeful. I can't help the smile that overtakes my face.

"Yeah, Johnny. Things are great."

His smile is tentative, but he lets me gather everyone in front of the van.

"Are you taking it with the Polaroid?" Gonzales calls out to John.

John gives him a deadpan look and shakes the camera in his hands.

"I literally don't know what that means," Gonzales whispers to me.

"That's his nice camera. Polaroids don't have timers and couldn't capture a high-quality picture," Aaliyah relays from beside him, discreetly wiping at her eyes. She must know John's never done something like this before.

"Of course," Gonzales says, nodding sagely.

John places the camera back on my dad's trashcan before rushing over to stand beside his dad at the other end of the van.

"Everyone say cheese," he calls.

We all smile as the camera goes off.

"How'd it turn out? Like something to remember?" I ask John, leaning against his shoulder to look at the screen.

He grunts and starts walking away.

"We should go before we miss our reservation at the campsite," he shouts over his shoulder.

I can't help but grin at my emotionally constipated boyfriend. Baby steps.

"Good thing Gonzales is my shoe size," he says as he hops into the van and tosses his bag in the back, on top of his new hiking boots.

"Yeah, good thing," I say, waving goodbye to everyone as I pray I remembered to take off the tags.

As soon as we're on the highway, Inu comes up to the front and sits in her dog bed in front of John's feet.

There's an exit to a pit stop just a few miles away and I smile to myself. When I first started on this van, that's all John and I were. A cold, unwelcoming pit stop that people are dying to get out of the second they step into it.

But now.

I look over at John, Inu's head in his lap as he pets her, gazing out the passenger window at the trees that fly by.

Now, we're everything but a pit stop. A place I'd like to stay in forever. Cozy and warm but still learning each other.

His skin glows from the dappling sun shining through the trees and I follow my desire to reach out for his hand.

"I've never been to a National Park. Even if it's just for Christmas break," he admits.

I squeeze his hand. "I'll take you anywhere you want."

異体同心

Acknowledgments

Woohoo! Another book that has entered the world thanks to so many magnificent people.

I'd like to thank my brother for so many things including being my sound board every time I needed to know something about Isamu being in the military. My parents for supporting me as I semi-quit my job to do nothing but write. Thank you to everyone who read this book just because they support me: DCT, Hannah Joy, Maddie, Ester, and Ryley. Your feedback was fantastic and kept me going every time I thought about throwing in the towel.

A special thank you to all my sensitivity readers. Trey, who helped me bring John to life and still owes me a few rounds of League. Kai who brought John's transness into a new and beautiful light. Kpyaman who became an expert in Isamu and his romantic gestures. Kendra Herber for teaching me things no amount of research ever could about Isamu's body. Hannah Joy, because Inu deserves good rep too.

My editors, Carmen Smith for helping weave together coherent ADHD thoughts and Jude Lee Baet for those pesky commas and pointing out my repeated words. My formatter Margherita Scialla for knowing how the heck things get formatted. I'd also like to thank Jess Joenck for appearing out of the ether to make amazing interior art as well as the cover.

Lastly, I could never forget to thank my cat, Calico Jack, who still lays on my computer while I work. Thanks for keeping my hands warm and my keyboard broken.

To my readers, I hope you enjoyed this book and it brought you some light to your life.

About the Author

Ellis Mae is an author based out of somewhere (they've moved more times than they can count and have probably already drifted somewhere new at the time you are reading this). Ellis enjoys skateboarding and hiking and laying in bed eating pretzels off their stomach. You can find them on their website ellismaewriting.com, instagram ellismaewriting, or at random independent book shops.

They've also written The Hills We Run From, a sapphic story based out of Edinburgh, Scotland.

9 7 9 8 9 8 7 3 1 0 6 2 5